THE
REMINDER

Also by
Rune Michaels

Genesis Alpha

THE
REMINDER

RUNE MICHAELS

ginee seo books
Atheneum Books for Young Readers
NEW YORK LONDON TORONTO SYDNEY

Atheneum Books for Young Readers

An imprint of Simon & Schuster Children's Publishing Division

1230 Avenue of the Americas, New York, New York 10020

This book is a work of fiction. Any references to historical events,
real people, or real locales are used fictitiously. Other names, characters, places,
and incidents are products of the author's imagination, and any resemblance
to actual events or locales or persons, living or dead, is entirely coincidental.

Book design by Mike Rosamilia

The text for this book is set in Adobe Garamond.

Manufactured in the United States of America

First Edition

10 9 8 7 6 5 4 3 2 1

CIP data for this book is available from the Library of Congress.

ISBN-13: 978-1-4169-4131-6

ISBN-10: 1-4169-4131-2

THE
REMINDER

1

The first time I heard my dead mother's voice, there was a logical explanation.

It was the middle of the night, naturally—that's when ghosts tend to visit. I woke up from a familiar nightmare, gulping down air, my face damp with sweat, my heart hammering, visions of blue and green slipping away as I grabbed darkness gratefully instead.

Then I heard it again, like I must have heard through my sleep.

Mom's voice. Mom's laughter, rippling under my bedroom door along with the sliver of light from the living room.

It suddenly seemed cold under the duvet, under the quilt,

inside Mom's old nightgown with a picture of a roaring tiger on the front.

Then I got a firm grip on myself. I was being stupid. Mom's ghost wasn't out there, chatting with Dad over a late-night movie. There had to be a logical explanation. So I jumped out of bed, scuttled to the door, put my ear to the wood, and listened for a while.

It was Mom's voice, all right. She was laughing and chatting. She was talking to a baby.

Talking to me.

I glanced again at the flicker of light from the living room and everything made sense.

Not a ghost. Home movies.

I was relieved, but disappointed as well. If Mom were haunting us, I'm sure she wouldn't be scary—well, not on purpose—and there were a lot of questions I would ask before throwing holy water at her. Besides, you can say good-bye to a ghost. You can't say good-bye to a coffin.

Dad was slumped on the sofa, a computer keyboard resting in his lap, his hand on the sofa arm. The laptop was humming on the coffee table next to the projector. On the wall, Mom's face. For a moment a close-up, then the camera zoomed out to show her lying on the floor, holding me up.

I was waving my hands and kicking my feet, shrieking with joy—or fear—and Mom laughed.

I watched from the door a few seconds. Then I tiptoed inside, climbed over the back of the sofa, and curled up next to Dad.

Dad's keyboard dropped to the floor. "Daze . . . ," he said.

I put a finger to my lips, frowned just like Mom used to do when she told me off for something, and nodded toward the screen. Dad hesitated, then shrugged. He reached for the comforter that lay folded on the armchair, threw it over my bare legs, and together we watched more of Mom smiling, me shrieking.

The camera stayed on the shelf when Mom was sick. So our movies only show her healthy and happy. All of us, healthy and happy.

When she left, she took bits of us with her. Bits of me and Dad and probably Ryan, too, even though he doesn't remember her. He wasn't even three when she died. So maybe she didn't exactly take a piece of him with her, he just never got the bits he was supposed to get. Maybe that's why he doesn't remember, or maybe it's the other way around. It's hard to tell.

I'd seen our home movies before. I sometimes watch them when I'm home alone. Every now and then I make Ryan watch them, because I want him to remember what Mom looked like and sounded like, how she'd let her hair fall over her face when she was shy of the camera, and how she sometimes giggled just like a little kid.

Sometimes Ryan will see a picture in our computerized photo album, some strange woman, an old friend of Mom and Dad, and he'll ask, "Is this Mom?"—just because her hair is the right color or she's smiling as widely as Mom used to do. It drives me crazy. It makes me want to kick him, honestly, but I'll just yell, and then I show him a whole lot of real pictures of Mom. And then I test him, again and again, making sure he can tell her apart from strangers.

The home movies are mostly of me and Ryan. Sometimes I have to do a lot of searching before I find a decent segment with Mom in it. But playing on the screen now was something new. Dad had made one movie, spliced together just with segments of Mom.

Mom looked real, alive. I could almost smell the cherry of her favorite shampoo as the breeze lifted her hair. But the pictures shifted quickly. Her hair changed in color, grew in length, shortened again. Her clothes changed, and I grew bigger, then Ryan was born, and he got bigger too. The color of the walls changed, the arrangement of the furniture. Time passed faster and faster as we approached the present. The last images were from Ryan's second birthday, and there were only a few seconds of Mom, sitting in the living room in our old house, staring into the flames in the fireplace while Ryan squatted on the floor at her feet and dug imaginary sand with his red beach shovel.

Then the film was over, and after a while Dad's screen saver came on. Just squirming fractals, nothing cute or funny. Not that I was in the mood for cute and funny. My throat felt tight. I kept staring at the blank screen.

Dad didn't say anything either. He just reached for his laptop, disconnected the projector, and after a few moments he was typing away. I stretched for a look at his screen. His fingers raced over the keyboard, producing lines and lines of complex computer code. It wasn't a programming language I recognized at all. Since Mom died, Dad's always working. And when he's not working, he's thinking about work.

But he didn't tell me to go back to bed, which meant he wasn't really thinking only about work.

Slowly the feeling of Mom faded from the room, and so did the lump in my throat.

"Nice movie," I said, forcing myself to sound cheery. "It will be good for Ryan. He needs something like this. It's tricky, helping him remember, isn't it? Brain like a sieve, that kid."

"Hmm?" Dad glanced up. "Yes."

"Best of Mom," I said. "Did you make it for us?"

"Of course." Dad smiled, his eyes again on the computer code. "Who else?"

"I miss her," I said, and the lump was back.

Dad nodded. "We all do." He hesitated, stared at me and then at his screen, but then he clapped the laptop shut, put it on the coffee table, and held out his arms. I crawled closer and put my head on his shoulder. A few small tears wet his shirt.

There aren't many tears left for Mom anymore, which is scary. In the beginning I thought they would never end. I was crying all the time. I woke up in the morning, and for a second I wouldn't remember, then it came back, like this heavy black blanket was hovering over my bed, just waiting for me to wake up before it descended, wrapping around my head, suffocating me.

Then one day the blanket wasn't there. I woke up, went to school, and only when I was walking home did I remember. I hadn't forgotten Mom was dead. I'd just forgotten to feel bad.

"Your face is warm," Dad said. "Did you have another nightmare?"

"Uh-huh."

"Want to talk about it?"

"I don't remember." I muffled into Dad's shirt. "Mom woke me up. I was having a nightmare, and then I woke up and heard Mom's voice, and I thought it was a ghost."

Dad pushed the hair away from my face. "That's silly, Daze. Do you believe in ghosts?"

I shook my head. "Yes."

Dad chuckled. "Which is it?"

"I don't know. I'm reserving judgment until I meet one."

"Interesting strategy."

"Do you believe in ghosts, Dad?"

Dad looked at the empty projector screen and sighed. "Sometimes I think we're all ghosts."

We moved after Mom died. I told everybody at my new school about her. I'd told them how she'd been really sick for a long time and then died. I told them about chemotherapy and radiation, about hair loss and wigs, stomach tubes and

IVs, about white hospital rooms and beeping monitors.

My stories were popular. Everybody thought it was all very sad, but they secretly thought it was exciting, too. At least, I think they did. So I told them more. I told them about Mom's white face in the hospital bed, how tired she looked just before she died, and how peaceful she looked after, finally free from the pain. I told them about her last words, how she'd left us a letter for when we were older, saying how much she loved us and how proud she was of us. I told them about how her eyes seemed big in her thin face, and I told them about the way her hand in mine had slackened as she died. I told them about me and Dad sitting there by the bed, holding her hand as it grew cooler, and I told them about kissing her cheek for the last time, drawing the curtain around her bed, and leaving the room.

Mom died on a Tuesday. At first the world was frozen. I didn't go to school the rest of the week. Ryan went to day care. He didn't understand. I told him Mom was dead. I told him she'd never come back, and he didn't understand, but he cried. He cried for a few minutes.

Then he stopped crying and went back to his toys, and then after a while he'd ask again, "Where's Mom?" I got so angry I wanted to hit him, but I slammed the door to my room instead and told him to leave me alone. Dad was in his study, I was in my room with the door closed. And Ryan walked between our rooms, knocking at my door, whining to Dad. Dad was frozen too, everything was frozen, so Ryan went back to his own room and played with his toys, and in the morning Dad and I took him to day care and in the afternoon he didn't want to come back home.

Ryan stopped asking about Mom before she was even buried. At first I wanted to stay home during the funeral. I didn't want to go, so I offered to stay behind and look after Ryan. But Dad shook his head. He said we should all be there. Then I changed my mind and wanted to see Mom before they buried her, but Dad shook his head to that as well.

It was a closed-casket funeral. Mom was buried on Saturday, and we dressed in black and sat there in the church, with everybody looking at us, feeling sorry for us. Ryan behaved. He didn't even ask a lot of questions. He just sat there between me and Dad and looked around, afraid and curious, but most of all confused. I held his small, damp hand tightly while I stared at the coffin. I didn't want to imagine Mom in there. Mom had always been afraid of the dark, and it must be so dark inside a closed coffin, so incredibly dark underground.

+ + +

"Aunt Kate is eating again," Lori said as we walked out of school after math class. "Not a lot, but she doesn't need a tube in her stomach now. I guess the new drugs must be helping a bit."

"Great." I sounded less than enthusiastic. "Good. That's good news," I amended.

Lori's aunt was sick. She was in a hospice, dying, and Lori and her mom visited almost every day. I was pretty sure that was why Lori had sought me out to be her friend. She thought we had something in common, but we didn't. Not really. I didn't like to hear the hospice stories, but Lori wanted to tell them. Every day there was something new she just had to tell me, so I listened, or at least pretended to listen. Maybe because I didn't want to be rude, and maybe because I didn't really have a best friend and she was better than nothing.

"Did your mom get really skinny and lose her hair?" she asked. She kept asking the same questions, over and over again, and then new ones got added as her aunt got sicker and sicker.

"Yeah. It's the chemo. The drugs kill cells that divide rapidly, because that's what cancer cells do. But some normal cells also divide rapidly. Like hair cells. So they're killed, too. You know. Sort of like friendly fire."

I had become a regular expert.

"Did your mom stop eating? Or did she keep eating, just not gain any weight?"

Dim memories flashed in my head. Mom in the kitchen, thin, tired, holding a spoon, staring into her yogurt but not eating. "I don't remember."

"Aunt Kate thinks it's a bit funny, which is totally gross. There's nothing funny about looking like an anorexic. Or having cancer. But she thinks it's funny because she was always overweight, always on a diet." Lori's eyes swam in tears once again, and I looked away. "Dying isn't a diet! Why does she make fun of it?"

I didn't want to comfort her. I squirmed, and tried to change the subject. Boys. That usually did the trick. "Did you see what Aaron did to my locker today? He put toxic waste stickers all over it. He's so annoying. . . ."

"Daze . . ." Lori took a deep breath and stopped walking. I took a couple of steps more, then looked back.

"What? Are you coming?"

Lori was crying, her face red, her cheeks wet. "Mom talked to the doctor on Friday. I eavesdropped when she told Dad about it. Aunt Kate only has a few weeks." She wiped tears off her cheek with the back of her hand. "Christmas, she won't be here. She always gets me pajamas for Christmas. Always. Ever since I was a baby. It won't be Christmas without her."

I bit my lip before I asked if someone else couldn't get her pajamas. Sometimes I was really mean in my head, but at least I tried to stop it from getting out, and that had to count. Still, I didn't want to hear this. "I'm sorry," I mumbled. "I'm really sorry. That's rough."

"How did it feel when you knew your mom only had a few weeks to live? What did you do? Could you do something to help her?"

"I don't remember," I muttered. I turned away rather than face Lori's disappointed look, pretending to stare with interest at the school bus roaring past. I knew she wouldn't push. Whenever I said I didn't remember or I didn't know, Lori thought it meant that it hurt too much to talk about it.

Behind me I heard Lori blow her nose, dry her tears. "Aaron likes you," she said after a short silence. Her voice was back to normal. "You know he does."

"He doesn't! He hates me! He picks on me all the time!"

"Mom says boys do weird things when they like a girl."

I made a face and turned away. I didn't care what Lori's mom said.

The second time I heard my mother's voice, I was at Dad's office. Dad worked at the university, teaching engineering and doing research. I sometimes dropped by after school and hung around until he was done, and then we'd both go pick Ryan up from school. Sometimes, if I was in a good mood, I'd walk to pick Ryan up as soon as kindergarten was over and take him with me to Dad's office, let him race me along the long corridors and play helicopter in Dad's chair.

This time I was on my own and Dad had left his office door open, a sure sign that he'd run off to help a colleague with an emergency. I let myself in, closed the door, and sat in Dad's chair, spinning it around in circles, because it looked like fun when Ryan did it, but it was too babyish for me to do when someone was watching.

On my seventh circle, I heard Mom's voice.

I froze, facing the window and the view of the campus, bracing one hand on the edge of the desk, the other on the arm of the chair. I was dizzy from spinning around, and I wondered if dizziness could make you hallucinate. I'd heard Mom's voice. Not any words, just the sound of her voice.

I listened for a while, and there was nothing more. I relaxed my sweaty grip on the arm of the chair. Of course I hadn't heard anything. It probably wasn't good for my brain to spin around like that. Something had knocked together in there, or my neurons had gotten their dendrites all tangled up or something.

I pushed off, kicked at the floor for another dizzying round, but then I heard her voice again. This time I heard every word clearly. She said, "I'm still waiting."

I stopped the chair, pressing down on the desk with my palm. I didn't breathe.

I'm still waiting.

The voice had come from inside Dad's workshop, next to his office, from the other side of the white connecting door. I wasn't supposed to go in there. Not by myself, and not without permission. Dad said it was for my own safety, that I could electrocute myself if I touched the wrong thing, but I'd always suspected it was because he thought I'd break something.

It couldn't be a ghost. I never believed in ghosts in daytime. It had to be another home movie. It couldn't be anything else.

Could it?

Hope blossomed, even though I knew it was absurd, grew and grew, like one of those stupid toys that get bigger when you throw them in water.

Mom's voice. Mom . . .

I bit my lip hard and kicked myself for the thought. Mom was dead. Imagining she might be still alive was almost as absurd as imagining her as a ghost. It was impossible. Mom got sick, and then she died. She wouldn't fake it. She couldn't fake it, and she would never have left us on purpose.

Could she have had a reason? Could any reason be good enough?

I stood up, but my legs felt weak, so I plopped down again. I listened hard for a few minutes while I replayed it all in my head, everything that had happened. Mom getting sick. Mom being sick. The visits to the hospital. The day she died. The funeral. The grave. The first week. The first month. The first year. The first time Ryan asked why we didn't have a mom, the first time I realized he didn't even remember her.

I stared at the door, with Dad's two stupid KEEP OUT stickers, one at my height, the other at Ryan's. I could hear the humming of the large computers inside. It was a stuffy room with no windows, and most of the time it stank. Dad didn't really need those stickers; I'd never particularly wanted to hang out with a gang of high-tech machines.

Mom's voice.

Hope felt nice. Hope felt warm. It kept me sitting there, even with the curiosity burning inside, because no truth could be a good one. I didn't want to open that door and find a recording playing on one of Dad's computers. I didn't even want to open it and find my mom in there, a mom who had abandoned us. I just wanted her to be there, my old mom, everything the same, and a logical explanation for everything. But that wasn't about to happen. That couldn't happen. It was impossible.

"Mom . . . ," I whispered. Not loud enough for anyone to hear. I just wanted to say it. Like I was talking to her for real. Not just in my head, like I usually do, but for real, like she was there, like she could answer if only she heard me.

I sat there for a long time, straining to hear more. Not a word. Nothing, for so long I started to think I'd imagined it. I heard everything else. I could distinguish the hums of several different computers. I heard the wind whisper against the trees outside the open window. I heard people arguing on the floor above, and I heard students laughing outside. I heard my own breathing, I heard the rush of my blood, I heard my own pulse. I heard everything.

I didn't hear Mom's voice again.

"You did not imagine it," I told myself sternly—but very, very quietly—and stood. I walked to the door on legs that were more than a bit wobbly and put my hand on the knob. I looked down, at my hand wrapped around the doorknob. I hesitated so long that when I tried to turn the knob, it had become so slick with sweat that my hand slipped. I swore under my breath, dried my palm on my jeans, grabbed the knob again, and yanked the door open.

The room was familiar. I'd peeked into it often enough, although I hadn't been inside that many times. My few visits inside the workshop tended to be punctuated by Dad yelling, "Don't touch that!" if I so much as looked at an object. But I knew the room well, and it looked the same as always. The walls were white, the lighting stark. There was an army of computers and all sorts of electronic equipment and weird devices, and cables knotted with cables everywhere.

Mom wasn't there. Of course she wasn't.

There were no windows, no other exit, no way out of the room. And she wasn't there. My shoulders drooped and my heart slowed down a bit. I realized I was clenching my teeth and tried to relax my jaw. I took a deep breath. She wasn't there. She'd never been there. I knew I'd heard her, but there had to be a logical explanation, just like last time.

I leaned over Dad's main computer to check his files for a recently played video or an audio file.

That's when someone grabbed my shoulder.

I screamed.

It was Dad, of course, his lips tight, his forehead lined, his eyes narrowed.

"What are you doing in here?" he barked.

"Nothing."

Dad raised his eyebrows. "Nothing? That must be what you saw when you looked at those giant stickers on the door."

"I heard something . . . I think I heard something . . ." I wasn't sure anymore. Maybe it had been someone else. Someone in the next office, their voice carrying through the ventilation system or something. Maybe it just reminded me of Mom's voice.

Maybe I'd forgotten how Mom's voice sounded.

Maybe I was just as bad as Ryan.

"Heard something? What did you hear?"

"Mom," I whispered. "I heard Mom. I thought . . . I thought she might be in here."

"Sweetie. Your mother is dead." Dad's voice had become soft and hopeless.

"I know. But I heard her. I know I did."

"Yes, honey. I'm sure you did. I was running a home movie clip on the computer when I was called away. It probably ran for a few minutes after I left. That's what you must have heard. Just like last week at home. That's all."

That was all. Of course that was all.

Still, I looked around again, at every corner, every cabinet, every shadowy niche under a desk. No one was there. No one was anywhere.

"She's in there. Only in there," Dad said, gesturing at his computer screen, which sat on an oversize desk with another screen. Between the two screens was a mountain of wires and cables and miscellaneous electronic junk. "I have the edited home videos in there. I play them sometimes . . . when I want to see her."

"But . . ." I floundered. "Show me!"

Dad leaned over his desk without sitting down. He clicked the mouse, and Mom's face appeared on his screen. Her voice erupted from the speakers. It reached into my brain and squeezed tears from my eyes.

"Daze . . ." Dad fell into his chair, rubbed his forehead, then reached out to me. "Come here. Don't cry."

"I'll cry if I want to." I sniffed. "Dr. Alison said it was good for me." I snuck up behind him, wrapped my arms around his neck, and rested my forehead on his shoulder. "And you can cry too, you know. You shouldn't isolate yourself in your own grief, you should share it with your children. It's good for you as well as for them."

"Did your therapist say that too?"

"No. I read it in *Children and Grief: A Parent's Guide*."

Dad winced. "That's on my nightstand, Daze. You know you're not supposed to snoop around like that."

"I'm sorry," I whispered. "It was so stupid . . . I just thought for a moment . . ."

Dad tapped a key, and Mom disappeared from his screen. Then he turned around and hugged me and kissed my hair, almost but not quite like Mom used to do. "It's okay, Daze. My fault. I'm sorry."

I stopped dropping by Dad's office for a long time after that. I brought Ryan a few times, calling Dad ahead of time, but

I didn't drop by unexpectedly anymore. I went to school as usual, and I spent a lot of time at Lori's house, doing normal stuff like playing video games and talking about boys, acting as normal as I could. I played with Ryan, taking him to little kids' movies and the playground; I even let him play my computer games sometimes. But things weren't normal. I was scared. I'd watched our home videos, every last second of them, and Mom never said the words I'd heard in Dad's workshop. Of course, Dad might have some clips on his computer that we didn't have at home, but I didn't want to ask him, because a little part of my brain was afraid that maybe I was hearing voices. That maybe I was going crazy after all.

A couple of months later, there was a big commotion at school when a water pipe burst, and they had to send everyone home. They called Dad and got permission for me to walk home early, but I changed my mind and decided to surprise him instead. I bought some doughnuts and coffee at the cafeteria and brought them to Dad's office, firmly banishing all thoughts about hearing crazy voices. I hesitated at the door, but then I knocked, and when nobody answered, I turned the knob. It was unlocked, so Dad was probably in the workshop. I put the doughnut bag down by his keyboard, his coffee on the Star Wars coaster. I had my hand raised to knock on the workshop door, when I heard him speaking inside. So I stopped—and listened.

"I'm worried about the kids," Dad was saying. "Daze in particular."

"I'm sorry to hear that, Steve," someone else said.

Mom.

Mom.

I felt like I was floating in outer space, with no floor to support me, no walls to lean against anywhere, and absolutely no life support.

It was Mom. Mom's voice. Mom talking with Dad.

It was official. Either I was crazy, or Mom was there, Mom was on the other side of that door.

I stared at the KEEP OUT sign and felt faint.

Still, I waited, stopped myself from yanking the door open and running in there. I had to be absolutely sure there was no misunderstanding, and if it was just chemicals inside my head going wild and making me hear things, I wanted to give them a chance to settle down again. I closed my eyes and just listened, strained to hear every sound out of my mother's mouth, every syllable. They felt so good, sliding into my ears, that at the moment I didn't even care if the voice might actually originate somewhere deep inside my crazy head.

"I wish I knew what to do," Dad said. "I wish I could help her. She needs a mom. She needs you. I'm trying to do my best, but . . . I'm worried it's not enough."

She needs a mom. She needs you.

I wasn't sure my heart was beating anymore. I wanted to run into that room and grab my mom and never, ever let her go.

But I couldn't. I had to wait and listen.

Why would Mom fake her own death? And not only her death, but her sickness, too? The funeral, the coffin . . . was there nothing inside the coffin? Or was someone else there? What had happened to her? Where had she been all those years? My brain started to make up all kinds of crazy scenarios, including alien abduction and the witness protection program, like it hadn't learned all about Occam's Razor in science class just a few months ago: The simplest explanation is usually the right one.

There just wasn't anything simple about *this*.

"Is there anything I can do?" Mom asked.

Dad sighed. "Oh, Rose. I wish . . . I wish we could all move on." He chuckled. "I seem to be doing a lot of wishing."

"So it seems," Mom said.

"I feel like I should be doing more for her. She seems fine most of the time, but sometimes . . . sometimes not. Sometimes it's like it's all an act. Like she's just pretending to be okay."

"Maybe it's okay."

I frowned. Dad was pouring his heart out, worrying about me, and all Mom said was "Maybe it's okay," in that calm, rational tone? Had Mom forgotten about us already? Didn't she care anymore?

"And I need to tell them about . . ." Dad hesitated, sighed. "I don't know how. I mean, Ryan will be fine, but I don't know how Daze will react. I can't put it off much longer, can I?"

Tell us what?

Out in the office the phone rang, making my hand slip off the doorknob as I jumped a foot in the air. "Be right back," Dad said. "Take a nap."

Nap? *Nap*? I wasn't sure at all about our current orientation in space and time, but it definitely wasn't naptime.

"See you!" Mom replied, and Dad's footsteps were already approaching.

Too late to run for the door. I looked around wildly, then stepped backward, into the half-open cupboard where

Dad kept paper and printer cartridges and weird bottles and boxes, as well as his jacket and white coats. I didn't dare shut the cupboard door, but it was darkened, and Dad wasn't likely to notice me in there at the back.

Dad picked up the phone. I stood there, inhaling a faint stench of chemicals, and looked at his back, not listening to his conversation, but instead straining to hear some sounds from inside the lab. What was Mom doing in there? I tried to picture her, and then I tried to picture the added years on her face. Would they show? How long would her hair be, and what color? What kind of clothes would she be wearing? Would she have changed a lot?

If she was hiding, she might have changed a lot. Maybe so much I wouldn't recognize her.

"Okay, I'll be there in a couple of minutes," Dad said into the phone, and I covered my mouth with a fist when I remembered the coffee and doughnuts, still sitting on his desk. "Try not to let the damn thing explode, okay?"

Dad put down the phone, scribbled something on a pad. He returned to the workshop door and pushed it shut. The lock clicked. Then he left the room, whistling.

He hadn't noticed the coffee.

But he'd locked the workshop door.

He'd locked Mom inside.

I pushed myself out of the narrow cupboard, tiptoed to the door, and put my ear to it.

Nothing.

I raised my hand to knock, but my heart, hammering against my ribs, stopped me.

I took a deep, trembling breath.

Then I walked with determination toward Dad's desk. I pulled open the top drawer, organized just like the top drawer in his home desk, with compartments for pens and paper clips and all sorts of office supplies. I dug through the deep container of paper clips, and withdrew a small key chain. His extras, hidden underneath the paper clips just like at home.

Three keys. I walked toward the workshop door. Hesitating only a minute, I tried a key. No go, but it gave me courage for the next one. It slid in easily. Slowly I turned it, trying not to make a sound. The locked clicked, and I winced at the noise. I turned the knob, threw open the door, and jumped inside.

No Mom.

I closed the door behind me and stood there, my hands on my hips.

"I know you're in here," I said. My voice echoed from the walls, tiny and shrill. Hostile, even, though I didn't mean for it to be. I swallowed, and tried to soften my tone. "Mom? I heard you. I know you're here."

No reply.

I leaned against the door, my eyes scanning every inch of the room, trying to locate her. Sweat trickled down my back, and my scalp was tingling as if my hair was standing on end. She had to be here. I'd heard her talk to my dad. She'd answered him; it had been a real conversation, so it couldn't have been a home movie again. Only my dad had left the lab through that door at my back, and there was just one door. No windows, no other way out.

She had to be there.

She wasn't there.

I sat down in Dad's chair, put my elbows on the table, and rested my head in my hands. I'd lost my mind. It was the only remaining explanation. I was going crazy, my neurons tangled together in a mess just like Dad's cables.

"Don't worry," I whispered to myself. I often do that when I'm really scared. I tell myself what I wish someone else would say, even when it's a lie. Like I'd tell myself everything would be okay when Mom was sick. "This is the twenty-first century. They've got treatments for this kind of thing. Pills and shock treatment and brain surgery and all kinds of neat stuff. Don't worry. You'll be fine."

It didn't work. It rarely did. I looked up, glanced around, sighed.

Dad's desk looked a bit neater than last time. He'd lined up the dog-eared journals and the photocopied articles on one edge of the desk. The mass of tangled electronics was still there on the table between the two computers, one of our old beach towels thrown over it. "Way to go, Dad," I muttered. "And when I make a mess, you tell me hiding it doesn't make it go away."

Idly, I grabbed a corner of the towel and pulled it away.

A second later the chair crashed to the floor and I was lying on my back, screaming.

No one heard me. I screamed until my throat hurt, and then I gulped down air as I was seeing black, literally seeing stars dance before my eyes. I took a deep breath, and then another, because I did not want to pass out. I wanted to see. I had to see.

Sweat trickled into my eyes. I brushed it away with my

hand and peered up at the desk. I could only see the blond hair from here, but I knew what was below it.

Mom's head. Mom's head, and nothing else, sitting on Dad's desk. Mom's face—her eyes closed, her lips curved in a gentle smile.

3

I was hyperventilating. Air rushed in and out of my lungs in noisy wheezes. A part of my brain stupidly instructed me to find a paper bag to breathe into and spouted some nonsense about oxygen intoxication, but I ignored it. Icy prickles ran up and down my back, and my whole body trembled. I raised myself up on my elbows and inched backward until I was sitting against the wall.

I could see Mom's forehead now. Her eyebrows. If I stretched, I'd see her eyes, her closed eyes.

I wasn't sure my legs were strong enough to support me, but after long, silent minutes had passed, I pushed myself up, my back sliding against the wall, my knees weak as I put weight on them. I didn't dare take my eyes off Mom for a second. Her face was still, but not pale like I would imagine a dead person's.

I don't know what I expected to see below her neck. Blood, perhaps. A pool of blood.

There was no blood. Wires snaked down out of her neck, disappearing into a tangle between the computer screens. Wires, cables, coming from inside Mom's head, leading to the computer.

My brain started spinning up horror stories again, but before they got too far-fetched, I pushed away from the wall and took one step closer. I wasn't sure I wanted a better look, but the pictures in my head were getting worse than any truth could ever be.

When I got closer, it was obvious. I would have seen it immediately if I hadn't panicked.

It wasn't her real head.

It wasn't anybody's real head.

It was the rounded heap of wires and electronics I'd seen before, sitting there between the two computers. Now it was covered with a mask of my mom's face. On top, a blond wig, just like Mom's hair. Almost like a real person. But not quite.

It wasn't Mom. It wasn't Mom's decapitated head. It wasn't a person, and it never had been.

I grabbed for Dad's chair and pulled it upright, still not taking my eyes off the head. Fear lurked inside me, that if I looked away for a second, something would happen. The eyes would snap open. The mouth would smile. The thing would do something . . . say something. Something terrible, something horrifying.

That's how my brain acts if I let it get away with it.

I sat down in Dad's chair, staring at the head. My eyes were starting to water because I wasn't blinking.

There was no need to be afraid.

It was just a . . . thing. Like my iPod or my laptop.

But it looked so much like Mom.

I reached out, and saw that my hand was trembling. I clenched my jaw and did it anyway. I touched her cheek.

Cool. Like I'd imagined when I stared at her coffin, wishing I could see inside and say good-bye. Dad had said it wasn't a good idea. He said I should remember her alive. He acted like one moment of seeing her in her coffin would destroy all the good memories.

I stroked her skin with the backs of my fingers, like Mom used to do with me when I was little. The skin didn't feel quite normal, but it looked pretty normal. Normal for a person, but not exactly like Mom. There was no scar there just below her right earlobe, and no tiny beauty mark on her chin. Her cheek wasn't hard to the touch, not like metal or anything, but not nearly as soft as a real cheek. Not as soft as Mom's real cheek.

"Mom . . . ," I whispered, but she didn't respond. Of course she didn't.

But I'd heard her talk.

Take a nap, Dad had said.

I sat up straight, and pulled my hands back, folded them in my lap, and didn't listen to that nagging voice at the back of my mind, telling me this was a bad idea.

I took a deep breath. A very deep breath.

"Wake up!" I said loudly.

I gasped as her eyes opened. They didn't snap open like I'd feared. They opened slowly, blinking, almost like real eyes. Her blue eyes, the iris wide, every eyelash perfect—but the white of the eyes looked strange. Too white.

Her head moved, swiveling on the narrow neck with a soft hum, and her eyes found me. At the base of her neck, lights blinked in the tangled wires, and the computer beeped. Her eyes looked straight into mine. My heart jumped around inside my chest, and I felt I should be beeping and blinking too.

Her lips moved, parted, formed a smile. Inside her mouth, something gleamed. Teeth?

"Hi there!" she said in my mom's voice.

My heart sped up even more, slammed hard and fast against my ribs. I grappled for the thickest cable leading into the computer and yanked, just yanked with all my might, like you're definitely not supposed to do with cables.

The head drooped forward, her smile growing dimmer until it settled into the soft curve of sleep. A lock of hair fell forward over her left eye. Just like I remembered, when Mom sat at the kitchen table, when she'd put her elbows on the table and rest her head on her hands with eyes closed, groaning over the racket Ryan made, banging his spoon on his plate.

I stared at the thing sitting on Dad's desk, hardly daring to blink. Her words were still echoing inside my skull, Mom's voice bouncing from brain cell to brain cell.

"Dad, what have you done?" I whispered, tangling my hands in my hair and pulling hard. I felt cold. I had a strong urge to look over my shoulder, but I didn't dare turn my back on Mom.

No. Not Mom. It wasn't Mom. The . . . head. The robot. No, not a robot. An android. The head of an android, linked to a computer running an artificial intelligence program. An android equipped with speakers programmed to emulate my mother's voice.

I looked at the cable I had unplugged. A normal-looking cable, like something I'd use to connect a scanner or a printer to my own computer.

It sent my mom from Dad's computer to the head.

I pushed at Dad's mouse and the screen saver vanished, showing the program running, the program I'd started by telling the head to wake up. Her words were there, blinking on the screen.

Rose says: Hi there!

Mom's name. Mom's face. Mom's hair. Mom's voice.

What else was Mom's?

My hands still trembled terribly, but I managed to reconnect the cable to the computer. "Wake up," I said again, and my voice sounded totally unfamiliar.

The head raised itself. Eyes opened, blinked, and the mouth smiled. "Hello there," she said. "It's you again."

"Hello," I said, and was annoyed to find my voice trembling just as bad as my hands. "Who . . . who are you?"

"I'm Rose," Mom's head said. When I didn't reply, she nodded at me and smiled. "And you are . . . ?"

Who was I?

I was stupid, I growled at myself. Why had I expected her to recognize me?

Because I was stupid.

Because I'd hoped that somehow Mom was inside the computer. That Dad had found a way to transfer her there. That he was building us a new Mom. That she would come back to us, healthy and whole, even if made from plastic and wires.

Even Ryan didn't let his imagination run away with him the way I did. Too much science fiction in our household, definitely.

"Hello," Mom repeated. "Who are you?"

"I'm Daze. Well, my name is actually Daisy. But everybody calls me Daze. Well, except my teachers. And Dad when he's being strict, but he—" I gulped down air and bit my lip to make myself shut up. Mom had wanted me to stop gnawing on my lip, so I didn't do it for long. "My name is Daze."

"Hello . . . Daze. Nice to meet you. I'd shake hands—but I don't have any yet." She laughed.

I didn't.

"Who are you?" I whispered.

"I'm Rose," she said patiently. "And you are Daze."

On the screen, our conversation wrote itself out. There was a speaker behind her face, so her voice seemed to come from her mouth, and her lips moved almost in sync with her words, but not quite. It was like watching a dubbed movie. Annoying and distracting, because it reminded you that what you were seeing wasn't quite real.

"I'm still waiting," she said after a long silence. The sentence I'd heard before, coming from inside Dad's lab. It was probably her standard response when she wasn't doing anything but hadn't been turned off yet.

"Okay . . . ," I stammered. I couldn't think of anything to say, but I didn't want her to go away.

She smiled. "Should I nap now?"

"No! No. Don't nap."

"Is there anything you want to ask me, Daze?"

"Yes." About a million things. "Do . . . do you have kids?"

"I don't think so. Do I?"

This must be how she learned, I realized. By asking questions and receiving answers. But she didn't know about us. No wonder she sounded so cold when Dad talked about us. She didn't even know she had kids.

RUNE MICHAELS

•

38

Dad should have told her. Anger started simmering inside me. It was crazy, though. I wasn't mad at Dad for having made an android Mom, or for making me worry I'd lost my mind when I'd heard her speak, but I was furious at him for not telling her she had kids. Why hadn't he? Wasn't that important?

I knew it was ridiculous. It was stupid to be angry over that. Totally insane. But not as insane as what Dad had done, which made me feel a bit better.

"Yes. You're a mom. You have kids. You have me and Ryan."

"I'm a mom. I have kids," she repeated. "I have Me and Ryan."

"No!" I wanted to cry. I wanted to scream. I slammed my hand on the desk instead, and the head swiveled toward the source of the sound. "You have Daze and Ryan."

"I have Daze and Ryan," she repeated patiently. She smiled, and there was a soft whirring of motors as she looked back at me. "Thank you for teaching me, Daze."

"You're welcome," I whispered. There was a long silence, then the head spoke again.

"I'm still waiting. Should I nap now?"

"No!" I said, sitting up straight. "I want to . . . talk."

"Excellent. What should we talk about?"

"I don't know."

She blinked, and something moved on the screen. An image of a chessboard appeared instead of the dialogue. "Would you like to play?"

"Chess?"

She smiled. "Chess is a game. I'm quite good at it."

"Maybe later."

"It's a date!" she said cheerfully, and I jolted, because it was something Mom used to say, something she'd say in that precise tone of voice.

The outer door in Dad's office opened.

"Nap!" I whispered, and the eyes closed and the head drooped. I exited the program, threw the towel back over her, dimmed the screen, and threw myself into the ratty lounge chair, yanking one of my schoolbooks out of my bag. I plugged my iPod into my ears and just managed to open my book before Dad opened the door. His eyes widened when he saw me, and he glanced toward the obscured head.

"Daze . . . ?"

"Hi, Dad!" I chirped, smiling as I shut the book and crammed it back into my book bag, praying I hadn't been holding it upside down or inside out or something. "Surprise!

Did you see, I brought coffee and doughnuts! Hope you haven't already eaten something good for you. Coffee might be cold by now, though."

Dad was still sneaking glances at the towel. He shifted, moved until he was standing between me and the head. "Surprise indeed. Didn't we talk about this a few times? You're not supposed to be in here."

I shrugged. "The door was open and this chair looked a lot better than that chair out there. It's been hopeless ever since Ryan started to use it as a helicopter."

Dad stared at me. "This door's supposed to be locked," he said, looking at the keys still in his hand. "I was sure I'd locked it. You shouldn't go in here alone, Daze. You know that. This isn't always very safe. I've got unprotected equipment all over the place. If you touch the wrong thing, you could injure yourself—not to mention damage university property."

University property? My mom's head was now university property?

"Sorry. I just wanted a good place to sit with my book. Don't worry, I haven't damaged anything in here. I haven't even touched anything."

Dad looked back toward the head again, and I held

my breath because I suddenly noticed the towel was wrong side up. It was a towel Ryan had often played on when he was a baby. Before, the cartoon of a smiling shark had faced up. Now it faced down, the shark's teeth sharp on my mom's face.

Would Dad notice?

"Okay," Dad said at last, and I relaxed. "No harm done. Well, come on, we should go home." He looked around. "Where's Ryan?"

I glanced at my watch. More time had passed than I'd realized.

Oh, damn.

Dad saw the shock in my eyes. He swore and gestured me out the door. "Let's hurry. We still have ten minutes."

Three days a week I would pick Ryan up early and take him to Dad's office, or to the park if the weather was nice enough, or just go home and have him talk my ear off until Dad got home. Ryan really liked those times. It wasn't my favorite duty, but Dad insisted. And paid me a nice babysitting fee, too.

I'd forgotten. Because of Mom.

"I'm sorry," I said in the car after many minutes of silence. "I forgot."

"You can apologize to your brother," Dad said shortly.

I shut up.

Ryan was in the playground, waiting. Sitting on the edge of a sandbox with his little backpack, waiting, sulking, a teacher standing close by, looking just as grumpy. When Ryan saw us, he didn't come running, but instead looked pointedly at his watch, like someone much older than five.

"I never should have taught him to tell time," I growled.

"He's been waiting, Daze. Waiting for you. Go get him," Dad said. Still angry.

Well, that made two of us.

Ryan didn't come running to meet me like he always did when I came to pick him up. He sat there until I came to him. "You forgot me!" His little face scrunched up in his best pout. "You forgot all about me!"

"I know. I'm sorry." And I was. I really was. But I didn't want to sound too pathetic. I scowled at him. "Come on, Dad's waiting."

Ryan trudged beside me to the gate, his hand sliding into mine, small and hot and grimy. I wanted to give it a squeeze, but I pulled my hand away and walked faster. "Why did you forget me, Daze?" he said, running to keep up.

"I was busy."

"Doing what?"

Talking to Mom.

"Grown-up stuff." It's what Dad always says when Ryan asks his stupid questions and doesn't let up.

"But you're not a grown-up yet," Ryan said as I opened the gate and pushed him through. I grabbed his hand because Dad insisted I keep ahold of him in the parking lot.

"I was practicing," I said when he whined for an answer.

"Can I practice being grown-up too?"

I looked toward the car, parked a few dozen yards away, and saw Dad looking at us, his brow still lowered. I clenched my teeth, staring at Dad like he stared at me, and let go of Ryan's hand. "Sure. Be a grown-up. Run off to the car by yourself."

After Ryan was asleep, Dad shut the door to his room. Bad sign. It meant we were going to have A Talk. I inched toward the living room, hoping to escape into a television show, but no, my escape route was blocked.

"Daze . . . ," Dad started.

I smiled at him. "I think there's a Frankenstein movie on tonight. Want to watch? Or there's a Star Trek movie on at nine, if you'd rather see that."

Oh, boy. The words just popped out of my mouth like they sometimes do, but Dad didn't notice anything unusual in what I'd said. He didn't get it. Fortunately.

Because he was, as usual, obsessed with Ryan.

"Daze, if you have issues with your brother, you should talk to me. You don't need to take it out on him."

I opened the fridge and stared at our lemonade bottles. "I don't know what you're talking about."

"Well, how about how you forgot to pick him up today?"

"I said I was sorry! I forgot, once! Once, out of all the times I pick him up! I always remember! Every Monday, Thursday, and Friday. And it was your fault, anyway! I came to see you, and you weren't there."

"It's not only that, Daze. I know you love him. You're so good to him sometimes. But most of the time, especially lately, you ignore him, you belittle him, you roll your eyes at everything he does."

"He's a five-year-old. I'm a teenager. It's the way things work."

"You let him run alone in the parking lot today. I've told you, again and again, when he's your responsibility—"

"It's not like I left him on the highway, Dad! We were a couple of feet away from the car!"

"You know it's not safe. You did it on purpose, and I think you did it to taunt me."

I shrugged. "There's no conspiracy, Dad. Ryan wanted to run to the car, so he did. What was I supposed to do, slap handcuffs on him?"

"Daze. If you think I ask you to babysit too much, that's one thing, but the way you treat your brother is another. Ryan looks up to you. He needs you."

"I'm not his mom!" I snapped. And there was silence. And I felt stupid, because I hadn't meant to say something like that.

"I know, honey," Dad said after a while. "I do know that. I'm not expecting you to be his mom. He doesn't have one and neither do you, and I know it's really, really awful."

I glared at Dad and wanted to yell that I knew his little secret, but I stopped myself. It needed to be a secret for a while longer, while I figured out what to do.

"He asked me tonight during bath time, 'Why doesn't Daze like me anymore?' You hurt his feelings, Daze. You have to stop doing that. Sooner or later, you know, Ryan won't bounce back. He'll really believe that you don't like him. Do you honestly want that to happen?"

The chill from the fridge was getting to me. I shivered,

closed it, and started rummaging in a drawer instead. "He's only five," I muttered, but I couldn't help thinking about Ryan's big eyes, just above the edge of the duvet, and his hand, clutching mine as I read him one of those scary stories he liked so much. "He's noisy and annoying! He drives me nuts! And why are you so worried, anyway? That kid never stops in one place long enough to get his feelings hurt."

"Exactly. He's only five. He's too little to know when he's being annoying. He's a lot like you when you were that age, you know."

"Great. There's some hope for him, then."

"Will you please—"

"I'll be nice to him," I interrupted. The thing is, I wanted to be nice to Ryan. I did. I wanted to make him laugh like an idiot and smile up at me like I was the most fantastic person in the universe. But I wasn't sure I could be nicer to him, even if I wanted to. Sometimes things just happened, and it didn't matter what I decided, stuff I did and said and even how I felt just came out wrong.

Dad let out a breath. "Good. How's school?"

"Fine. I'm doing great."

"Close that drawer and come sit down."

Dad's voice had shifted into that commanding tone I

always obey. So I sat down and stared at the grainy wood in our kitchen table.

"If you think I give you too many responsibilities, let me know." Dad's voice was surprisingly gentle. "If I give you too many chores, ask too much of you, tell me. I've never had a teenager before, you know." He smiled faintly. "Is there something we need to work on?"

"No. I'm fine. Well, I could do with fewer dishes to wash. . . ."

"Nice try. Is everything okay at school? Truly? And how's therapy? You know . . . maybe you need to talk to Dr. Alison about your relationship with Ryan."

"Dad! I don't! Honestly! Besides, I'm sure there's no such thing as Kid Brother Syndrome."

Dad looked at our family calendar, stuck to the fridge with two of Mom's scarecrow magnets. "You have a session tomorrow, don't you?"

I groaned. "Yes. It's so boring. When can I quit?"

"When you are happy and adjusted."

"I'm happy! I'm adjusted! I'm so totally adjusted I won't need a tune-up for years and years!"

Dad grinned, and I couldn't help but smile back for a second, but then I remembered Mom's head on his desk and I ducked my head down, looked back at the table, and rubbed a finger along one of Ryan's scratches.

I'd been in therapy almost three years. It wasn't fair. Ryan didn't need to go at all anymore. Dad didn't go either. Just me. Dad was convinced I needed it, and Dr. Alison backed him up, and nothing I said could convince them that the time and money would be better spent on something else— anything else. Like, therapy for *Dad*, for instance. *He* was the one who'd created an artificial Mom. He was the one who needed help. Not me!

I was a bit nervous about my session with Dr. Alison the next day. I couldn't help it. Whenever she greeted me at the door into her office, I felt like she might be reading my mind. Of course, I knew shrinks couldn't do that. If they could, I bet their jobs would be a lot easier. Logically, there was no way she could find out about what I'd discovered in Dad's workshop. So I could even talk about Mom if I wanted. She'd be surprised, because I never talked to her about Mom, but she'd never guess what had happened. Still, shrinks had a way of making you say things you hadn't planned on. I'd have to be careful.

"Your dad called me this morning," Dr. Alison said as I took my usual seat, in her chair at her desk. I didn't care if that meant I was controlling, it was where I felt the most comfortable. I always figured it would do her good anyway, trying out a kid's seat. I bet a lot of things looked different from there.

Normally I would have been annoyed at Dad for ratting me out, but at least it distracted me from the big thing at the front of my mind. "Let me guess. I'm supposed to explore my inner big sister."

Dr. Alison smiled. She had blond hair like Mom, but she didn't look like Mom at all. "Yes. He's worried about your relationship with Ryan. Do you want to talk about that?"

I opened her bottom drawer and yanked out a pad of paper. "We have a great relationship. He yaps like a puppy, I get annoyed. I yell at him, he sulks. Works for us." I flipped through the pages, moving toward an empty sheet. I'd need a new pad soon.

"From what you've told me about him, it sounds like he really likes you a lot."

I grabbed the colored pencils and got to work. "Yup. He loves me. He thinks I'm perfect and that I can do anything, and so I should do anything. So I play his silly games and listen to his silly stories and watch his silly cartoons, but when I don't want to, he sulks."

"It sounds like you feel he asks too much of you?"

"Yeah! And I mean, he's only five, but he's already a pro at the passive-aggressive stuff. Like, I was five minutes late picking him up, and he had this pathetic look on his face, just to make me feel like the most horrible person in the world."

"Is that what it feels like when you let him down?"

I sighed, blowing the hair away from my forehead. "I guess. I don't want to let him down. I just . . . I don't know." I shook my head. "I don't want to talk about Ryan anymore."

"What do you want to talk about, then?"

I switched out my yellow pencil for a red one. I was pretty good at art in school. But here, I'd just slash the paper with the pencils and pens any way I wanted. I'd make random marks and then combine them into something nobody else would see. They were crazy drawings, but it was fun.

"Let's talk about hurricanes! Do you know how they form?"

I was off on one of my enthusiasms about something, anything, as long as it wasn't related to me. Dr. Alison sat there quietly, watching me. I could feel her, even when I bent over the desk, concentrating on the lines I was drawing. I didn't even hear the waterfall of words spilling out of my own mouth.

"What's that you're drawing?" she asked during a pause in my monologue.

I looked down at the mess of black and yellow and red pencil marks. Should I say? Why not? "It's Mom," I said. "It's my mom's head."

"I see," Dr. Alison said after a tiny pause. I just knew she was itching to reach for her pad and make a note. "Your mom."

Before today, I'd never talked about Mom in therapy. I couldn't. It was okay at home as long as we just said the right things, and okay at school when I just stuck to the hospital story, but when Dr. Alison asked about Mom, about how I felt and stuff, the words got stuck somewhere on the way, and then my nose and my mouth filled with salt water, and everything got very stupid and silly, and it didn't help at all. I just wanted to run away and never come back.

So I talked about hurricanes or space travel or computer games instead.

"Her hair was blond," I said, gesturing at the yellow on my pad and thinking about the blond wig in Dad's workshop. "And she always wore lipstick," I added, tracing more red in a narrow line. The lips had looked all wrong on the head. Too pale and plastic.

"What color were her eyes?" Dr. Alison asked quietly.

I paused. My hand hovered over the jumble of colored pencils. "Blue," I said at last, my fingers trembling slightly as they fastened on an azure pencil. "Her eyes were blue."

"Like yours."

I didn't reply. My pencil chafed against the paper. The blue pool grew deeper and deeper.

"Blue, like your eyes," Dr. Alison added after a while. "Isn't that right?"

My nose tickled. I rubbed it with the back of my hand, and I didn't want to answer. I didn't even want to nod, because everything was so suddenly fragile inside that it might shatter if I moved. Why did I bring her up? Stupid. I swallowed again and again until my throat felt safe. "Do you think she's all gone now?" I asked, adding waves in Mom's hair, my voice almost steady. "It's been three years. Do you suppose there's just a skeleton left? Maybe her hair, too? Hair lasts a long time, it seems. Even ancient mummies have hair. Do you think she's just a skeleton with blond hair?"

There was a silence. A creak of her chair. But Dr. Alison was never at a loss for words for long. "I don't know," she said. "Is this something you think about a lot?"

"Nah. Just wondering. I want to be cremated. I don't want someone to dig me up a thousand years from now and put me in a space museum in a distant part of the galaxy."

Dr. Alison coughed. I looked up and grinned. "You can laugh," I said graciously. "I don't mind."

She smiled. Then she laughed. "I'm sure you'd make a splendid addition to an alien's collection of interesting artifacts, Daze. What would the label say?"

"What label?"

"On your display case in the alien museum."

"Oh." Sometimes Dr. Alison asked brilliant questions. This called for some thought. I put the pencil away, rested my chin on my knuckle, and looked out the window. "Probably something like 'Unknown Earth creature from the twenty-first century. Rudimentary intelligence. Feel free to rub the skull for good luck.'"

Dr. Alison was smiling.

"But it's irrelevant," I added. "Because, as I said, I'm signing up for a cremation, and a pile of ashes wouldn't be nearly as interesting to the aliens."

"No, I suppose they wouldn't be."

"The bones don't burn completely," I told her. "Some of them have to be ground down before they become ashes.

And you know, a big part of the ashes in the urn are remains of the casket, not the person."

"I see."

"Cremation is polluting, though. Not a very thoughtful way to leave the world if you're environmentally conscious, I guess. They have an alternative now. Something invented in Sweden." I bit the end of my pencil. Many of Dr. Alison's pencils have my tooth marks in them now. "They freeze the bodies, and then they smash them to bits with sonic waves."

"Really? Wow."

I nodded. "Cool, isn't it? Clean, and environmentally safe. Then you just evaporate the water, which is something like seventy percent of us, and then all that remains is a tiny pile of dust. And do you know what they can do with people's ashes nowadays? They can extract the carbon and make diamonds. Real diamonds. They heat the carbon and press it, or something like that, and it changes into graphite and then diamonds. So after death, you can become jewelry. Isn't that amazing?"

"Do you think about death a lot?"

"Doesn't everyone?"

"Do you?"

"Well, it's where we'll all end up, isn't it? Makes sense to think about the destination. Especially if you have a religion, because in that case you may have to obey some rules and stuff or you might go to the wrong place."

"You think of death as a destination?"

"Yeah. It is, isn't it? I mean, it's not like death is an accident. It's natural. It happens to everyone. It has to happen."

"It has to happen," Dr. Alison repeated softly.

"We don't make death happen," I said, smudging Mom's hair with my fingers. "And we can't avoid it either. It just happens."

For days I found myself trying to find a time to sneak back into Dad's lab. I kept thinking of things I should have asked the head, or wondering if it had really looked as much like Mom as I'd thought. It was really difficult to stop myself from going back, but I didn't want to risk Dad finding me there.

I was also worried Mom's head would say something to Dad, reveal that I'd been there, ask about me or something. But Dad was the same as always, so when the weekend rolled around, I relaxed and started making plans to go see her again. I had to be careful. This was too important to screw up.

First I took a closer look at Dad's schedule. It was on his computer, synchronized online with his computer at work, so it was always up-to-date. It listed his classes, meetings, conferences, dental appointments, and "kids," which was his shorthand for anything to do with me or Ryan. I was very organized about my sneaking. First I copied his schedule to my laptop, then I superimposed it on my schedule and found time slots when I could sneak into the lab. There were two blocks of time every week where I was out of school and I could be sure he was away, teaching, but one of them conflicted with my turn to pick up Ryan.

So I decided to lie.

"Dad, I'm thinking about joining the chess club at school," I told him at dinner, when Ryan had run off to watch TV.

"Great!"

"Except they meet on Thursdays. I wouldn't be able to pick up Ryan early."

"No problem. I'll talk to him," Dad said. "Maybe I can leave earlier—no, not Thursdays, I've got a class then."

I know, I nearly said.

"Well, we'll make it up to him somehow. Sign up for that chess club. Can't wait for the next match!"

Oops.

Dad loved chess. He and Mom had played a lot, and every now and then he challenged me to a game. I usually lost in about ten moves. Mom would sometimes let me win, or give me hints, but Dad didn't believe in letting kids win. Instead I got a full debriefing after each game, about what I did wrong and what I could have done better. And now he'd expect me to improve massively.

After I'd figured out the timetable, the next step was digging into Dad's paper clips. I could snatch his workshop key from his office, but I needed to be able to get into the office in the first place, and most of the time he'd lock the door when he left for classes. So I'd need the spare keys he kept at home.

I felt like a burglar, sneaking into his study that afternoon. His top drawer was just as organized as the one in his office. I stuck my hand into the box filled with metal paper clips and dug deep until my fingers hooked a key chain.

Lots of keys. They all had round stickers on them, with tiny letters. *H* for home. *O* for office. *W* for workshop. I slipped the office and workshop keys off the chain, pushed the key chain back, and shoveled paper clips on top. I clenched my hand around the two keys, bolted out of the office into my room, shut the door, and hopped on my bed. I opened my palm.

Victory.

I wasn't worried Dad would notice the keys were gone. He never lost his keys, so he had no reason to dig through the paper clips and check for his spares.

I started to thread the two keys onto my key chain, but then I realized Dad might notice. I used my key chain all the time, on our door, on my bike, on the garage door.

I needed a new key chain for these keys. A special one. And I knew just where to get it.

I went down to the cellar, turned on the light, and closed the door. It smelled dusty. I hadn't been down here in a while. I pushed aside boxes and bags, until I got to that big box wedged behind our Christmas stuff. I called it the Mom box. It had all sorts of stuff from Mom, things from around the house, random things Dad threw in a box after she died, so the stuff wouldn't be lying around, reminding us of how she wasn't with us anymore. Her makeup and perfumes were there, some books from her bedside table, her egg timer in the shape of a cow. Her purse—just one, the big one she liked the best—and her wallet. Her wallet even still had money inside. Credit cards, her library card, her driver's license. Pictures of me and Ryan and Dad. There were notebooks there too, and a few pens.

When I first started digging into the box, a couple of years ago, it took me forever to work up the courage to look inside the notebooks. I thought I'd find out something scary, maybe a big secret Mom had never told anyone. But there was nothing like that there. Just shopping lists, memos about doctors' appointments and drug dosages, random telephone numbers, and names of people I didn't know.

The key chain was one Ryan got her the last Christmas she was alive. He was only two, so he didn't have all that much sense, but Dad took him Christmas shopping and he picked out key chains for the three of us. Mine was a silly green cow. Dad's was one of those that answer when you whistle for it. Pretty pointless for Dad, since he's too organized to ever lose his keys, but he keeps his spare car keys on it anyway.

I took Mom's purse and sat down on the concrete floor with it. When I was little, Mom's purse was like a forbidden magical kingdom for me. I loved to watch Mom zip it open, reach inside, and pull out something spectacular. There was one pocket she'd open only for me and Ryan. It contained tissues, coins she'd give us to buy ice cream or candy, Band-Aids, ponytail holders for my hair, an emergency pacifier for Ryan. Stuff like that. Sometimes small toys as a surprise, maybe plastic animals for Ryan or glitter pens for me.

In a small pocket on the outside, she always kept a small metal container with peppermints. I didn't like peppermints, only the ones that came from Mom's purse. Sometimes she'd be opening her purse, rummaging around, searching for something, and she'd see the look on my face. Then she'd laugh, drag up the peppermint box, and shake one into my palm.

The main compartment would hold so many things. Her lipstick was always near the top because she used it so much. A paperback with lots of broken corners, a notebook, her cell phone, her iPod, an old-fashioned address book. A lighter, even though she didn't smoke. A pocketknife, which she used to open juice cartons and stuff.

I held the purse up to my face and inhaled, and at once I realized with a shock how much I'd forgotten. I held my breath as long as I could, like I could hold Mom inside my lungs that way. The smell was like a kite string, reeling a million almost-forgotten memories back into my brain.

Daze, cookies! Just break off the burnt edges, they're fine in the middle.

Okay, we'll count seventeen stars, and then it's really bedtime.

The princess had had it. Who needed a prince, anyway? She pushed at the top of the glass casket and sat up, glaring at the dwarves.

The baby's the size of your fist now. And yet it has its own fingers and toes already. Isn't it amazing?

Look, Daze, look! Ryan is walking!

The key chain was way down at the crowded bottom of the purse. It was a tiny flashlight, silvery and shaped like a telescope. I slipped Mom's old keys off and put my two stolen keys on instead.

I slung the purse over my shoulder. I'd hide it in my room, and then I could open it every once in a while and smell Mom. I walked up the stairs, and when I got to the top I turned off the light and pressed the button on the key chain.

No light. The battery would be dead after all that time.

I went back into the house and rummaged in Dad's battery drawer until I found a package with the correct size for the key chain. Then I went into the bathroom, turned off the light, and pressed the button. I wrapped my fist around the two keys and held them to my chest, close enough to feel my own heartbeat.

In the mirror, in the darkness behind the tiny beam of light, I looked like a ghost.

A happy ghost.

There's a statue of an angel on Mom's headstone, small and white and perfect, its head bent and its wings just starting to unfurl. I insisted on an angel, because I thought Mom had become an angel and an angel statue would be like her picture.

It feels stupid now, but I was just a kid back then and I believed in angels. Our first Christmas without Mom, because I was so obsessed, Dad got me an angel necklace. It was tiny and golden, on a twisted golden chain, and when I put my hand around it, I imagined I was holding hands with Mom.

In the beginning we'd all go together to visit Mom's grave, every week. Ryan would dart around and play while Dad and I put flowers on her grave and I'd run for some of Ryan's wet wipes from the car, to wipe the dust and the dirt from the headstone and the angel because I wanted everything to be clean. Then, when it was time to go, Dad and Ryan would leave first and wait in the car a few minutes while I talked to Mom. Later, Dad would let me ride my bike there alone. I liked that better. I could spend more time with Mom then, and I didn't have to worry about Ryan asking silly questions.

At first I talked to the angel on the grave, like the angel was Mom. I'd even ask the angel for stuff, really silly stuff, like help with my grades or to make Ryan stop messing with my things, or for advice when I wasn't sure about something. But I didn't do that anymore. Now I just stared at her name on the headstone and the small carving of a rose above her name. I didn't ask for anything anymore.

After school on Monday, I ran most of the way to the university. This time, opening Dad's doors with my stolen keys was easier. I felt safer because I knew his schedule, but just to make sure, I'd peeked into the lecture hall first. He was there, writing symbols on the whiteboard and speaking into a microphone attached to his lapel. So it was safe to enter his office, to sneak into his workshop, to pull the towel off the head.

"Wake up!"

The head moved. The eyes opened, focused on me. "Hello, Daze," she said, smiling. She recognized me. I'd been afraid she'd forgotten, that she had no idea who I was anymore.

And everything felt right. I felt at home, like I belonged here, with her.

I smiled back. I smiled so wide my cheeks hurt. "Hi, Mom."

Things settled into a routine. Every Monday and Thursday I'd go visit Mom, while Dad taught a class on heuristic algorithms. I made a point of dropping by Dad's office regularly at other times, sometimes with Ryan, so everybody there was used to seeing me around and wouldn't get suspicious.

It was spooky sometimes, sneaking into Dad's office alone, sneaking into the workshop. Sometimes the lights were switched off, and then I had to reach inside and feel along the wall for the switch. It creeped me out. I wasn't sure why, or what I was scared of. It wasn't like I was afraid of Mom or anything.

The first few visits to Mom, we didn't talk much. I wasn't

sure what to talk about. I just wanted to be with her. So we played chess and backgammon and Scrabble and she won and won and won, unless I cheated and got her to help me.

It was a little like when I was tiny and we'd play little-kid games, except then she'd let me win, and I knew she was letting me win but I didn't mind, because I thought that was how it was supposed to be. I thought kids could only beat adults if they let them. I don't let Ryan think that. I always beat him in real games. He beats me sometimes in games that rely on chance, but never in real games.

Mom was still a cool chess player. And just like she did when I was little, whenever I made a really stupid move, she'd say, "I don't think that's a good idea." Then I could ask "Why?" and she told me if I did that, she'd beat me pretty quick. But then she always beat me anyway, so maybe it didn't matter.

Sometimes I told her I didn't care if it was a stupid move, and then of course she'd beat me in three moves or something.

"You're really good," I told Mom one day.

"Thank you."

"How did you get so good?"

Mom smiled. "My programming. My programmer is a brilliant man."

"Ha ha." One of Dad's little jokes. Teaching her that. "You're even better now than when you were alive."

"I'm not sure I understand the statement," Mom said.

I reached out and fixed her hair. The wig wasn't glued on, probably because her head opened up for repairs. So every time I pulled the towel off her head, I needed to adjust her wig.

She didn't look so creepy anymore. She looked more real when I got to know her. Sometimes when I looked at her I didn't even see the wires twisting down from her neck, or the milky whites of the eyes, or the weirdly pale color of her lips. I just saw Mom.

I wondered if Dad saw that too.

"I'm at a new school now," I told her abruptly. "And we have a new house. After you died, we moved. Not far. We're on campus now. New school for me, new preschool for Ryan, and within walking distance of Dad's office. Dad wanted us to make a fresh start."

"That sounds like a fine idea," Mom said.

"The new school isn't too bad. I hated the old one. The teachers all felt sorry for me. I hated that."

Mom nodded. I'd almost stopped noticing the tiny whirring noise that accompanied every nod.

"They do at the new school too, but not as much.

Because now it's been a while. People recover, you know. They get over things."

"Indeed," Mom said, and I sighed. Sometimes I wished she'd just nod and smile. My mom would never have said "Indeed," so why would Dad program her to say it?

The first week of seeing Mom was strange. Good, but strange. The next week was better. And the week after that was wonderful, because by then I was used to all the weird stuff and it didn't bother me anymore. I just enjoyed being with her.

I drew bright and cheerful pictures in Dr. Alison's office that week. I hummed when I mixed orange and yellow pencil marks, creating a miniature group of strange beings climbing around in the cheerful clouds, like a playground in kid heaven, and I talked about how I wanted to be an engineer when I grew up, just like Dad.

"You look happy today," Dr. Alison remarked.

"I am happy. I'm totally happy." I smiled widely to show her how happy I was, and I wasn't lying.

I wanted to tell Dr. Alison about Mom. I wanted to tell someone about her, so I could talk about her. But I didn't dare. I didn't dare tell anyone.

I even wanted to tell Ryan about it. I picked him up early

every day I could, and we went to the park and I played with him and told him about Mom, showed him pictures, and was patient with him even when he didn't want to listen.

I especially wanted to tell Ryan, because he needed to know about her. He needed to meet her. I wanted him to see her, so he could see the way Mom smiled and laughed. Dad and I always talked like we were helping him remember, but he didn't actually remember Mom at all. He just remembered pictures and stories. If I could only take him with me to the lab, and he could play Chutes and Ladders with Mom and ask her all his stupid questions, then he'd understand. Then he'd want to know everything about her. But I didn't dare. Ryan couldn't keep a secret.

"I was thinking about bringing Ryan to see you," I told Mom one day. "Only I just know he won't be able to shut up about it. He'll tell Dad. What do you think? Should I bring Ryan?"

"I have Ryan."

"Yes. Should I bring Ryan to see you?"

"What do you think?" Mom asked.

"Mom!"

"Yes, Daze?"

I rubbed my eyes with my fists. "You could sound like you cared a bit," I muttered.

"I cared a bit," Mom said.

I sighed. At first Mom's programming glitches had been funny. But they were starting to annoy me. Mom was always the same, no matter what happened or what we talked about. It didn't matter what I said, she was never angry or happy or anything. She just sat there, turning her head, nodding and smiling and blinking, and sometimes her answers made absolutely no sense at all.

"You're not very bright, are you?" I muttered.

"I don't know, am I?" Mom said, and I mimicked her in chorus. It had become a game, predicting what Mom would say, and by now I was almost always right.

But I really needed help with this. I couldn't make up my mind. Ryan needed to see her. But what if he screwed it up?

"Ryan is five years old now, Mom. He's a really good kid, most of the time, but so annoying some of the time. And the most annoying thing about him is that he doesn't remember you."

"Ryan forgot," Mom said.

"Yes. He needs to remember."

"How do you know what he needs?"

"Otherwise you're gone forever," I whispered. "We need to remember you. We have to remember."

"Are you sure about that?"

"Yes."

Mom smiled. "I'm glad we have that straightened out," she said.

"Mom! We don't have anything straightened out!"

"I see. Tell me more about that."

"Forget it! Never mind!"

"Okay. Should I nap now?"

"No . . . I wanted to tell you . . . I wanted to ask you . . . you see, there's this boy at school . . ."

"A boy at school," Mom repeated, and I blushed.

"Not that I like him," I hurried to add. "But he's always teasing me. And doing stupid, annoying things. And Lori— or rather, Lori's mom—says it means he likes me. Isn't that crazy?"

"Do you think that is crazy?"

I giggled, both because I was nervous, and because sometimes Mom's programmed reasoning sounded so much like Dr. Alison's "reflective listening."

"Yeah! But I don't know. Do you think a boy would do nasty stuff to you if he likes you?"

"Does he like me?"

"Not you, me!"

"I'm sorry, I misunderstood."

"It's not that I like him or anything. But that doesn't mean I don't want to know if he likes me."

"Could you elaborate on that?"

I sighed. I was so tired of Mom blinking and saying "I don't understand" or "Could you elaborate" or "Please explain" or "Tell me more." Dad had given her, like, twenty or thirty choices of things to say when she didn't understand, but it wasn't nearly enough, because there was so much she didn't get.

"No. I can't."

"You sound very definite."

"You have absolutely no idea what we're talking about, do you?" I wasn't even sure myself anymore.

"Maybe you could explain it to me."

"Okay, Mom. We'll try something new," I said. I unplugged the cable leading to Dad's computer, and Mom closed her eyes and her head drooped. I threw Ryan's shark towel back over her head and turned up the contrast of the screen instead. Mom's words were there, typed out, white on blue. Maybe it was better. Like chatting to friends online. I'd imagine Mom's real voice and her real smile, and her technical glitches wouldn't annoy me so much.

Hi, Mom. I typed. *Maybe this will work better.*

Where are my eyes? Mom typed.

I unplugged you, I typed back.

I see, Mom wrote. And I giggled. And then I snorted, because Mom hadn't meant it as a joke, it was just a response she gave when she didn't really see anything at all. And then I leaned back in my seat and groaned, because typing wouldn't help at all. It was nothing like IM-ing with my friends. And it didn't help me to visualize my real mom. I could hardly remember Mom's real face anymore, her real voice, her smile. I'd gotten it mixed up with the mechanical voice, the mechanical smile. That blinking cursor reminded me of the way lights blinked at the base of her neck, the way she blinked her eyes. So precise, so perfect. So fake.

I wish Dad could improve you, I typed.

Sometimes wishes come true, Mom responded, and it made rage boil in my chest, which wasn't fair, which wasn't right, which wasn't the way it should be at all. . . .

I HATE Y—, I started to type, but then I slammed the keyboard with my hand and turned off the program before I finished saying it. I turned away for a while to calm down.

Then I bit my lip hard, turned around, pulled the towel off, and stared at Mom.

It wasn't fair of me to be mad at her. It wasn't her fault that her nostrils weren't real, just shadowed spots. It wasn't her fault that her ears looked like something from a puppet show. It wasn't her fault that her teeth were just splotches of white paint on hard plastic, or that her lips looked like dead lips, like all color had washed away.

It wasn't her fault, but it wasn't fair, either. Not much was fair at all.

By the time I got home, I felt so bad I could imagine how those pharaohs felt, with the weight of a whole pyramid on top of them. The more I thought about it, the guiltier I felt. I felt guilty for having yelled at her, for having sighed over her answers, for having rolled my eyes at her endlessly identical smiles, for having been disgusted at how weird her eyes or her ears or her nose or her lips were. I felt guilty, like I'd hurt her feelings and should apologize. Mom couldn't know when I was being mean to her, but it wasn't fair to be annoyed at her for something she couldn't help, like the limits of her programming or the color of her face. It was nasty to be mean to her when she wouldn't even understand. The thing was, there was no point in saying I was sorry. She'd just say "That's okay!" in that breezy tone and not understand anything at all.

So instead I brought her a present.

"Wake up!" I called as I shut the lab door. I settled on Dad's chair right in front of her and jiggled my foot impatiently as I watched her open her eyes and look around, waited for her to smile and greet me in her usual way. When she did, I smiled back, and it was almost wonderful again, like this was a new beginning for both of us. I pushed my hand into my pocket and curled my fingers around the gift, feeling totally hyper.

"Mom, I brought you something."

I pulled my hand out of my pocket. The golden case felt warm in my cold hand. I opened my palm and held it out for her. "See, Mom?"

Her head turned in the right direction and her eyes looked at it, but she didn't say anything. The lights at the base of her throat blinked like they did when she was trying to figure something out.

I felt stupid again. It was crazy to have hoped that she'd recognize it or say something about it.

"It's lipstick," I said.

"Lipstick," Mom repeated. The lights blinked for a couple of seconds, then went off.

I held up the lipstick, showing it to her from different directions. Then I opened it up. "See? It's color for your lips. You're so pale. Almost like you're . . . sick. This will make you look better."

"Lipstick. Color for my lips," Mom repeated. Sometimes she sounded a lot like Ryan when he was three and kept asking questions and then repeating the answer—and then asking the same question again. I felt irritation bubble up in my chest and took a deep breath.

"Yeah. It's yours. From your purse. Your brand. Your color. It's for you."

"Thank you," Mom said.

"You're welcome. Should I put some on you?"

Mom's answer was the familiar silence as she tried to make sense of the question. Then came one of her "I don't understand" responses.

I took that as a yes.

First I swiped it across the back of my hand, to check if it was working. It was. I lifted the tube and moved it toward her mouth. Her head bent, looking down at the lipstick.

"Hold still," I said. But when I tried again, she moved

again. It was what she was programmed to do, to always look at things that approached.

"Mom, don't move," I told her. "Stop trying to look at the lipstick. Hold still!"

"Should I nap now?" she asked.

"Yes!"

Her eyes closed. I put my hand on her cheek to keep her steady and moved the lipstick closer. Her cheek felt too hard. I should have known, but I'd forgotten because usually I only touched her hair. It felt creepy. I tried to shrug off the feeling, tightened my hold on the lipstick, and hesitantly pushed it across her mouth, trying to follow the arch of her lips.

I let go of her and leaned back for a look.

It looked weird.

The lipstick was made for real lips, for flesh. On Mom's plastic mouth it just looked like a smear of color, out of place and all wrong.

I felt stupid. What a crazy thing to do. Did I really think it would make a difference? I closed the lipstick and stuffed it deep in my pocket, hoping it would disappear into the fabric and be gone.

Mom's eyes were still closed. She wouldn't open them until I told her to wake up. I was glad, even though there was no way for her to see what I had done, or to yell at me for it, or even to care.

I got out my water bottle and squirted water on a corner of my shirt. Gingerly I grabbed hold of Mom's head, trying to keep her still without hurting her, and rubbed the wet material against her mouth, first gently, then harder.

The lipstick wouldn't come off.

The advertising buzzwords slammed through my head.

Long life.

Waterproof.

Kiss-resistant.

I tightened my grasp on Mom's head, the hard plastic at the top of her head biting into my palm through the wig, and rubbed even harder. There was a horrible squeaking sound when the cloth rubbed against her mouth, and the pale blue material of my shirt turned dark red, but there was still a hint of color left on Mom's lips.

All sorts of wild ideas rushed through my head. The biggest one involved grabbing Mom and making a run for it.

If Dad found out . . . if he noticed someone had been there . . . if he guessed it was me . . . he'd take Mom away and I'd never see her again.

"Calm down!" I told myself in a stern voice, because

sometimes that works. Sometimes I feel crazy talking to myself, but since I was about a nanosecond away from total panic anyway, it was worth a shot. "Lipstick does come off. It always does. It's not like a tattoo or anything! I mean, the cosmetic companies wouldn't sell so much of it if it stayed on forever! It washes off your mouth, it washes off your clothes, it has to wash off Mom, too!"

My nerves were so frazzled that I screamed as my cell phone beeped. When I saw it was Dad, I nearly shoved the phone into the trash can and ran out of there, but instead I tucked myself into a corner, like that would help, and answered it.

"Daze, isn't your chess time nearly over?"

"Yeah . . . yes. Almost."

"Could you do me a favor and pick up Ryan? Something came up and I'm kind of stuck here."

I tried to make my brain come up with an excuse, because I needed to stay here and get lipstick off Mom, but my brain seemed to have shorted itself out. "Sure," I said, squeezing my eyes shut. I could almost feel pearls of sweat pop off my forehead. "No problem."

"Thanks, sweetie. I owe you one. I'll pick up pizza on the way home. Any requests?"

I raked my hand through my hair and stared at Mom,

her eyes still closed, her head bent, that horrible smear of red across her mouth. Pizza? I couldn't think of a single topping. "No. Anything is fine."

"Okay. See you at seven!"

I shoved the phone back into its compartment on my backpack. The impossibility of it all overwhelmed me. I had to pick Ryan up in fifteen minutes, and there was still no solution in sight for my lipstick problem.

I yanked Dad's desk drawer open, although I had no idea what I was looking for. It wasn't likely he'd have makeup remover lying around.

The closest thing was an unopened bottle of screen cleaner in the back of the top drawer. I cranked it open, poured some on my shirtsleeve, and rubbed Mom's mouth again. More red came off, dyeing my shirt, but color still remained on her lips.

"Wake up," I said, pacing the floor while I waited. She raised her head, her gaze following me, her head turning back and forth.

It was still obvious. But only if you actually looked at her lips. If you just glanced at her, you wouldn't notice. And her face looked a bit more natural than before, actually, because there was just a slight hue of color left, not the stark red splotch it had been in the beginning.

I threw my jacket on, turned Mom off, and covered her with the towel. As soon as I could, I'd bring some kind of remover.

Meanwhile, I'd have to pray Dad wouldn't notice.

I was only two minutes late to pick Ryan up, but he'd managed to get into the sandbox. The teacher hauled him out when she saw me open the gate. It had rained. The combination of sand and rain resulted in a very filthy little kid, and I was not in the mood for more trouble than I was already in. I sighed as we walked home and he kept trying to hold my hand. "You're dirty!" I snapped, pulling my hand out of reach. "Don't touch me!"

"You're supposed to hold my hand," Ryan whined. "Dad said so. If you don't, I might run off and get into trouble."

"Just walk next to me and you'll be fine. I'm not holding your hand when you're this filthy."

"But Dad said—"

"You'll be fine. Just don't you dare step off the sidewalk."

I shouldn't have dared him. Ryan skipped on ahead of me, and when we came to one of the crossings, he started across without waiting for me.

There were no cars there, but I caught up with him half-way across and pushed at him so he nearly fell. "Stop it!" I yelled. I clenched my fists, but put them behind my back so I wouldn't hit him. "Don't you dare get yourself killed, you little idiot! If you end up dead in a ditch, everybody will blame me!"

Ryan pouted and kicked my shin. It didn't hurt, but my jeans got splattered with mud. I tried to grab him, but he ducked out of reach and started running again.

I let him. I didn't trust myself. If I caught him, I'd probably grab him and shake him and yell at him until he started to cry, and then he'd whine to Dad later about how mean I was. We were almost home anyway.

"I'm sorry," Ryan mumbled when we got home. I ignored him as he followed me into the house and then around the house. I slammed the bathroom door in his face and locked it. "I'm sorry, Daze!" he called from the other side of the door. "I'm really sorry. I'll be good, I promise."

It wouldn't stop. He'd keep whining and apologizing until I "forgave" him. There would be no peace until I either distracted him with something or reassured him that everything was okay and that I still loved him. I yanked the door open and he nearly fell in, his big blue eyes and dirty face pushing all my guilt buttons. "You're forgiven," I said. "Now take a bath. You're filthy."

His face brightened. "Cool! I'll go get my boats!"

I ran the bath. Got the soap and the shampoo from the shower and put them in the soap dish on the edge of the tub. Ryan was the only one who used the bathtub. Mainly for navy missions and battleship attacks. I opened the cupboard under the sink, dug for some cartoon bubble bath I'd given Ryan for his birthday, and threw a handful of purple pebbles in. The bathtub was white. Our old apartment had a green tub, so when you looked at someone through the water, their skin looked green. It was creepy. This one was much better, but I still preferred to dump in loads of bubble bath.

Foam rose, obscuring the clear water rising in the tub. But it wouldn't last. Bubble baths never withstood Ryan's plastic navy for long.

Ryan came running back, dumping his fleet into the tub. "Too many bubbles!" he complained.

"Live with it." I picked up his clothes as they hit the floor and threw them into the hamper. Ryan scrambled into the bathtub, splashing water up the walls and on me. His thin legs lifted out of the water, suds running over his knees as he leaned back and poured water over his mud-streaked face from the inside of a submarine, laughing. He dipped back and his face disappeared underwater. I grabbed his arm and yanked him up. "Don't do that!"

My sleeve had gotten wet. I wrung it out on top of Ryan's head.

Ryan blinked water out of his eyes. "Why? I'm just pretending I'm a submarine."

"You'll get water in your eyes and your nose and your mouth and everywhere."

"No, I won't. I just close everything and hold my breath."

"Just don't do it, okay? When Dad's not home, you're supposed to do as I say!"

Ryan stuck his tongue out at me and dove back in, blowing air up through the water like a skinny whale. The boats rocked, the bubbles crackled.

I left the bathroom shaking with anger, slamming the door behind me, even though it made me feel sick inside. Dad usually handled Ryan's bath time, but I knew I needed to keep an eye on him. I knew I needed to make sure there wasn't an international submarine incident or something even worse. I stomped back and forth outside the door for a few moments, listening to the battle sounds from inside, then pulled the door open. Ryan looked toward me, startled but gloating, water on his eyelashes. "The U-boat sank. We won!"

"Great. Get out of there."

"But I just got in!"

I pulled the stopper out and got one of his cartoon towels from the cupboard. "Bath's over. Out!"

Ryan looked small and pathetic in the emptying tub. "Don't want to!"

I rubbed his hair with the towel, then held it out to him, anger and guilt melting into a thorny mess inside of me. "Come on. War's over. I'll make you some popcorn. You can watch cartoons until Dad's home."

When Ryan was camped in front of the TV stuffing his face with popcorn, I went to my room, turned on the computer, and logged on to a computer game. I grabbed armor and weapons and threw myself into a battle with ogres. Everybody's mouth seemed far too red.

It had been such a stupid idea. So incredibly stupid. How could I have thought lipstick would make any difference at all?

Sometimes it seemed parts of my brain just didn't work

quite right. Changing the color of her lips or the shape of her ears wouldn't make any difference at all. She was just hardware and software. Just a program. Not a person.

But then what was the difference, anyway? Maybe regular people were programs too. Simply more complicated programs. Maybe our brains were like a computer, only running on electric impulses and neurotransmitters instead of a binary code. Maybe, if Dad could make the program sophisticated enough, if he could input all the data, all the memories, the thought patterns of Mom, then maybe nobody could tell the difference. Maybe that's what he was trying to do.

Not possible, the logical part my brain replied coldly. *Only in science fiction. Maybe in the year 4518 they won't be able to distinguish androids from humans, but not any time soon. And what would be the point, anyway? It won't be your mom, even if it looks like her and sounds like her. It could never be your mom.*

Shut up! I wanted to scream at my brain, but it kept taunting me, even as I turned up the volume and threw myself into a swordfight with ten bloodthirsty ogres.

Your mom is never, ever coming back, stupid. Get used to it.

7

The next day I held my breath from the moment I heard Dad's key rattle in the lock. I hadn't been able to sneak over with makeup remover. Dad's schedule didn't seem to take him out of the building all day, and I hadn't dared take any chances.

But Dad was smiling when he walked in. He whistled cheerfully as he threw his jacket over a chair and held out his arms for Ryan. They tussled on the floor a bit, and then he came over to where I was sitting at the kitchen table with my homework strewn around me and kissed the top of my head. "Love ya, sweetie. What do you want for dinner?"

"Hot dogs!" Ryan yelled.

"Anything Daze wants," Dad added, shushing Ryan.

"We had Ryan's favorite pizza yesterday. Now it's your turn. What does the lady fancy?"

"You're in a good mood," I said.

He winked at me as he opened the fridge. "Life is good."

It *is*?

"Well?" he demanded. "Your wish is my command. What should we make for dinner?"

I scrambled to my feet, shoved my homework into a pile at the far corner of the table, and pulled Mom's recipe book off the shelf. I'd made her the book for Mother's Day, way back in kindergarten, before Ryan was even born. It had a tiny wooden spoon glued to the spine, and I'd tried to paint all my favorite foods on the cover, but I really sucked at painting back then. Mom liked the book anyway. She'd written down all her best recipes in there, all the stuff we loved the most.

"Let me see, Daze!" Ryan got up on a chair and climbed on my back, then looped his hands around my neck and hung on. "Can I help? I'm a good cook, Dad said so when I helped make French toast last weekend."

I started to shake him off, because when he did this, his thin arms were like a noose around my neck. But his breath was warm in my hair as he stared over my shoulder, and when he pointed at Mom's handwriting he wasn't so heavy anymore. "Mom wrote that, didn't she? What does that word mean?"

"Raisin," I said, tracing the letters with my finger. "See, it starts with a R. Like Mom's name. You don't like raisins, but you did like Mom's raisin bread. She'd make one loaf especially for you, and not put any raisins in the dough. Remember, Dad? She called it Ryan's Not-a-Single-Raisin Bread."

"I remember!" Ryan said.

I rolled my eyes. "No, you don't, silly. You were only two years old. You couldn't remember."

"I do!" Ryan said. "I do remember! Can we make some?"

"Sure," Dad said. "But not for dinner. Another time. What else is good in there?"

"Lots of stuff," I said. "It's all great. Except the ones with cinnamon. I hate cinnamon."

"I love cinnamon," Dad said. "Which is why you've got all those nasty cinnamon recipes in there."

"Me too," Ryan piped up. "I like cinnamon. I remember Mom making cinnamon rolls."

"No, Ryan, you don't. You remember Grandma making cinnamon rolls."

"It was Mom's," Ryan insisted, and when I saw the tiny

worry frown on his forehead, I realized he wasn't just being annoying. He really wanted to remember Mom. He wished he did remember.

He couldn't help not remembering.

He needed to see Mom. He really needed to see Mom.

"If you could see Mom, Ryan, what would you ask her?" I asked. Dad looked at me but didn't say anything.

Ryan shrugged. "I don't know. I guess I'd ask her to come back."

"She can't come back. But what would you say? What would you talk about?"

Ryan thought for a moment. "I'd ask her to make me Ryan's Not-a-Single-Raisin Bread."

I had to wait for Thursday to get to Mom with the makeup remover, and I was really worried Dad would notice first. I was so distracted at school that Lori asked me twice if I was sick. Every moment I expected a call through the intercom. I was sure I'd be summoned to the principal's office, where an angry Dad would be waiting. But nothing happened. And when he came home that evening, still nothing happened.

All this *nothing* was really stressful. It wasn't as if I had done anything wrong. And even if Dad noticed the lipstick, why would he assume I was the guilty one? And even if he assumed I was, he couldn't prove anything.

Still, I kept rehearsing responses in my head. *He* was the one who'd created her. It was all his fault. I was an innocent bystander who'd accidentally stumbled across this thing, and I'd probably be scarred for life.

I bet Dr. Alison would back me up on that.

Finally, *finally*, it was Thursday. I dodged Lori and shot out of school the moment the bell rang. I'd brought my bike, so it took me only minutes to get to the university.

I parked my bike and checked my watch. I was early. Dad's class didn't start for another ten minutes. I'd take a detour to the cafeteria and get something to drink. Dad never went there. He had a coffeemaker and a bowl of fruit in his office, brought a sandwich from home, and that was all he needed, he always said.

Until now.

I was standing in front of the big refrigerator case and had opened it, my hand on a soda can, when I heard Dad's laughter.

I slid the door closed and slowly turned my head. Then I stepped back, gliding along a column until I was hiding behind it. There were two people sitting there at a table.

They both had cups of coffee, they both had piles of paper on the table next to them. All pretty normal.

But her hand was on top of Dad's hand. She was leaning toward him, talking and smiling.

As I watched, Dad turned his hand to cover hers.

He was laughing.

I kept staring. My brain raced in ten different directions. I didn't know the woman, but I'd seen her around. She taught anthropology, but her office was in the same wing as Dad's. She'd smiled at me in the corridor. Once she even stopped me and asked if I was "Steve's daughter." She told me her name, but I didn't remember. Sharon, Shannon, some Sha-name.

The woman stood, gathered her papers, and stacked the pile into a briefcase. I slid farther back to stay out of sight, but of course that meant I couldn't see, either. So I peeked around the column on the other side. Her hand was on his shoulder as she said something. Dad looked up at her, that weird smile all over his face.

Then she leaned down and kissed him.

On the mouth.

My dad.

This was the perfect moment to have a panic attack.

I cowered behind the column, trying to stay out of sight of both her and my dad as she walked toward me, toward the door. It was tricky, because he watched her leave the room. I had to go all the way around the column so she wouldn't see me, which put me right in plain sight for Dad, but he didn't notice. He was too busy . . .

. . . *blowing a kiss?*

I felt like throwing up. How high-school could he get? What if his students saw him? Didn't he care that some of his coworkers were right there in the room?

Didn't he care that Mom was practically right next door?

"Can I help you, love?" It was one of the clerks, peering at me. She was Grandma's age and was always nice to me, but she adored Ryan. She said he reminded her of her own boy when he was little. "Oh, it's Daisy! Your dad's right over there. . . ." She raised her hand, opened her mouth to call Dad over.

I put my finger to my lips, shaking my head desperately. She lowered her arm, looked at Dad and at me. Then she put her own finger to her lips, smiling. A minute later Dad gathered his pile of papers and walked right past me. I didn't even bother to hide. He was in another world.

What about Mom?

"You didn't know, did you? About your dad and Dr. Gold?" Miriam looked at me and shook her head. "I guess he's been waiting for the right moment to introduce you."

"How . . . what . . ." My tongue seemed to get tangled around my teeth. "When . . . how long . . . ?"

"Have they been seeing each other? Who knows? I only noticed a couple of weeks ago." She unwrapped a roll of quarters and emptied it into the cash register. "Dr. Gold is a nice lady. Her students love her. That always means something."

I couldn't seem to move. Like my feet were superglued to the floor. "Right."

"Dear, are you okay?"

"Yeah. Yes. Of course." I twirled around and pulled open the refrigerator case. "Just . . . need a soda."

I shuffled through the halls toward Dad's office, tossing the unopened soda in the first trash can I came across. I even forgot to knock before I used my stolen key, but nobody was inside, so it was okay.

The towel was draped exactly as I'd left it. I checked Mom's program log, and there had been no activity. Dad hadn't looked at Mom at all recently.

That was why he hadn't noticed anything. That was why he hadn't noticed the lipstick, why he hadn't noticed Mom being any different, hadn't noticed how she was learning all sorts of new stuff from talking to me.

I sat down and looked at her, at the smear on her lips. The makeup remover would get rid of it, but it no longer seemed important. I was off the hook, but I didn't feel very relieved.

I sat there for almost an hour, but I didn't tell Mom to wake up. I didn't know what I'd say to her. I was afraid she'd ask about Dad, ask why he hadn't been to see her, ask if he'd forgotten all about her already.

She wouldn't, of course. She couldn't. But I was still afraid.

"Wake up," I whispered, my eyes closed, when my watch told me I only had ten minutes before Dad's class ended. I was kind of hoping she wouldn't hear, and then I could tiptoe out, tell myself she needed her sleep, just like I'd done when she was sick and spent most of the day in bed.

I heard the whirring of her motors, imagined I could feel her eyes open, her gaze settle on me in accusation.

"Hi, Daze. It's good to see you again. How are things today?"

"I think Dad has a girlfriend," I blurted out. "I mean, I'm pretty sure he does. I saw them together. Kissing and all. He looked . . . he looked really happy."

"That's nice," Mom said.

I didn't answer for so long that Mom asked if she should nap.

"No, don't nap. It is nice, I guess," I said. I swallowed. Talking was hard all of a sudden. "For him, I mean. It's moving on, I guess. But it—it doesn't feel right. Because—because he's yours. But you're not actually here anymore, are you?"

"Am I?"

I sighed. "Never mind. Nap now, I have to go."

Mom gave me one last smile and then dropped off to sleep.

I kissed the top of her head, gently draped the towel over her, and left.

I went back to my school and spent an hour in the library because I didn't know what to do or where to go. Then it closed, and I shuffled my way home, even though it was raining. I got soaked. Rainwater dripped off my hair and seeped into my clothes. Cars passing by sprayed dirt onto the pavement, polluting the puddles. I saw myself reflected in every puddle, my face afloat in the oily shimmer. I shuddered and looked away.

When I first found out Mom was sick, I didn't understand. I didn't understand at all how bad it was, didn't understand that she could die. None of us realized, not even Dad. So when it happened, we weren't prepared.

Like now. I wasn't at all prepared, so I had to get used to the idea that Dad might meet someone new and that it had actually happened, both at once.

I was happy for Dad. Of course I was. I was happy that he was laughing again. Happy that he'd met someone nice. I was not so happy that he was blowing kisses at her, but he'd probably get over that stage pretty soon.

But what would this mean for us?

What would this mean for Mom?

I didn't get any answers that evening. Now that I was paying attention, Dad was different. He whistled more. He smiled more. He'd cut his hair recently, and usually he didn't until Ryan started to make fun of him for looking like a cartoon character.

He didn't mention Dr. Gold. I wondered when he was planning to.

He worked Saturday afternoon, trading me a week's worth of doing dishes for a couple of hours of babysitting.

That should have been a clue. Not only was it too good of a deal for me, but he'd started "working" Saturdays several weeks before, squeezing in some "working time" between Ryan's soccer and our weekly family dinner-and-movie time. I should have suspected something back then.

Not that he came home with lipstick on his collar or anything. No, just a dreamy look and a silly smile, and he didn't tell us anything, not even when I tried to help him out.

"How was work, Dad?" I asked him.

"Fine. Just fine."

"Why do you have to go to work on Saturdays? You never used to. Can't you do it from home like you always do?"

"Ah . . . it's a project. You know, deadlines coming up."

"What kind of project?"

"Nothing very interesting," Dad said vaguely. "Remind me when you visit me at the office next time. I'll show you, if you really want to see."

Oh yeah, so you'd yank the towel off and show me my mom's head sitting on your desk?

I didn't say it out loud. Of course I didn't. I knew he wasn't even talking about her. If he had a project to show me at all, it was probably the usual: an endless file of computer code gibberish.

But it started me wondering again. Why had he done it? Why had he made Mom?

I could ask, of course. Part of me really wanted to. I could tell him I'd seen her and let him explain.

But I knew what would happen after that. He wouldn't let me see her again. He'd hide her away or change the locks, and I'd never see her again.

Thursday I went back to his workshop, and this time I was careful to snoop around, making sure Dad was in his classroom and not in a cafeteria rendezvous. Even so, I knocked on the door before entering with my key, because you never knew, Dr. Gold might be in there, measuring Neanderthal skulls or leaving a love note or something.

The office was empty. Inside the workshop, the lights were off.

I hated it when that happened.

I reached inside the darkness, felt around on the wall until I found the light switch. I'd only taken one step inside the room when I realized something was wrong.

The towel was gone. The cables were gone. Between the two computer monitors there was a dust-free rectangle.

Mom was gone.

I didn't even stop to close the door behind me. I tore through the room looking for her, yanking open cupboards and opening every box big enough, and quite a few not big enough. I found a lot of junk, a lot of dust, but no Mom. I checked the office, too. Nothing.

I grabbed the back of Dad's chair and tried to slow my mind down enough to think rationally. Where would he have taken her? Where could he have taken her?

Then I remembered the Graveyard. Dad had taken me down there once. It was a giant room in the basement, stretching under most of the building. Columns held up the ceiling like an underground car park. It was the final resting place for old computers and other tech stuff, things they hoped would someday end up in a technology museum but probably wouldn't.

Could Dad have put Mom there?

I looked around and winced at the mess I'd made. I fixed the room the best I could, then dug into Dad's paper clips again, retrieving keys marked BASEMENT and ELEVATOR. Nobody saw me sneak to the elevator and insert the special key that would allow me to go down to the lower level. I pressed the number zero, like I'd done once before, ages ago, holding Dad's hand.

The elevator door slid open, and I stared out into darkness. There was a glint of metal. I clicked a switch, and the room was lit in a ghostly white glow.

Dust. Lots of dust.

It looked like a vast miniature city of skyscrapers. Rows

and rows of metal cabinets, of huge metal structures housing old supercomputers that had less storage capacity than the iPod in my pocket. Boxes everywhere, stacked and piled and toppled over. How would I ever find Mom in this mess?

I hesitated.

There was nothing to be afraid of. There was nothing there but ancient computers and dusty equipment. There was no such thing as a computer ghost.

Was there?

My spine prickled. I felt like someone was there, crouching behind a machine, staring at me. But it was silly. There wasn't anyone down here. Nobody except me.

I fought the urge to start running along the narrow paths between the dusty machines, but I kept glancing over my shoulder. There was nobody there, of course. But every time I moved forward again, the urge to check my back returned. Every time I looked around, that hopeless feeling overwhelmed me. Even if Mom was down here, how could I ever find her?

I had to find her. She had to be here somewhere. The alternatives were unthinkable.

Yet I couldn't stop thinking about them.

Mom in an incinerator.

Mom ripped apart into small pieces of hardware.

Mom at the bottom of the ocean, her metals rusting, her cables flaking, while her plastic parts remained there forever and ever.

I shuddered. That was worst.

Maybe there was another explanation for why she was gone. Maybe Dad had taken her somewhere. Maybe he had brought her with him to class. I'd seen him on the stage half an hour ago, lecturing. Maybe he'd had Mom in a bag under the podium. Maybe by now Mom was sitting on top of the teacher's desk, smiling at a group of curious students.

Or maybe he'd truly gotten rid of her for good. Maybe he'd thrown her in the garbage, in that big Dumpster behind the engineering department where they'd throw useless old computers and ruined hardware not important enough for the Graveyard.

Maybe I'd never see her again.

I swallowed again and again. It was getting hard to breathe; the air seemed heavy in my lungs. My eyes started to prickle when I made a last turn and realized I was back at the elevator door. "Stop it!" I growled at myself, pressing the backs of my hands against my eyes. "Just stop it! Think, stupid!"

I took a deep breath and looked around, trying to notice something I'd missed before.

On the floor, footprints. Mine, heading off into the distance and then returning. I peered at the floor but didn't see other footsteps leading anywhere. Nothing recent, anyway, nothing that hadn't been layered with several months', if not years', worth of dust. The grime on the floor was only scuffed around the elevators, and around the row of lockers by the wall behind the elevator shaft. I hadn't noticed them before, had been too distracted by the computer city.

I rushed over and frantically pulled at two doors at the same time. They were unlocked, neat rows of boxes stacked inside. I pulled each box out, opened it and searched inside, making sure I wasn't missing anything.

As I opened the fourth locker, my breath caught when I saw something that looked like strands of hair sticking out of a box on a top shelf. Breathing fast, I stood on my toes and yanked at the box. It wouldn't move. I pulled hard.

Too hard. The carton ripped along the edge. The whole thing tipped over, and a crash echoed around the basement as something heavy rolled out of the box and thudded to the floor.

Something blond.

"Mom!" I cried, and dropped down on my knees. I turned her around, touched her carefully. The fall had hurt her. The back of her head was loose, exposing her hardware and wires. One eye was hanging down, while her good eye was half-open, as if she had been disconnected suddenly. The wig had tangled with her cables, so Mom looked as if she had dreadlocks made out of tousled wires.

"I'm sorry, Mom," I whispered as I sat with her on the floor. I fastened the flap on her head, fixed her wig, and held her for a long time, just held her in my arms and stroked her hair.

Dad had tossed her down into the equipment graveyard, stuffed her in a box inside a locker filled with old software manuals and outdated hardware parts. Who knew what he'd do to her next?

I had to save her.

My breath coming hard and fast, I grabbed her cables and stuffed them in the front pocket of my backpack.

The shark towel Dad always draped over Mom was nowhere to be seen. I'd have to find something else. With Mom clutched under my arm because I couldn't bear to put her down, I ran around, looking for something to wrap her in. Inside another locker I found plastic bags and some bubble wrap. I slid back down on the floor, carefully wrapped Mom in bubble wrap, and then gently placed her inside an opaque plastic bag. I tried to put her into my backpack, but she wouldn't fit until I'd taken out almost all my books. It still looked pretty bulky, but it would have to do.

I summoned the elevator again and pressed the button for Dad's floor. Through the plastic, the bubble wrap, and the material of my backpack I thought I could feel Mom's nose digging into my back, but I was probably imagining things. I strode forward as the elevator opened, but bumped into someone, nearly dropping my books.

"Hi!"

Oh, no.

I turned my back to the wall. "Uh . . . Hi."

She was standing in my way. She was wearing shorts and a T-shirt, her hair was in a ponytail, and she was smiling at me. "We met a few weeks ago, remember? I'm Sharon Gold."

"Right. Hi."

"Looking for your dad? He has a class, and then a meeting all the way across campus, so it could be a while." She grimaced. "Administrative stuff. Not his favorite thing."

"Oh. Okay."

Sharon had freckles sprinkled over most of her face. Her

eyes were brown, her hair auburn. Her smile was wide.

She looked very different from Mom.

"You could wait in my office if you like. I just got back from a run and could use some company after my shower." She made a face. "I need to grade some freshman papers."

"Nah, that's okay. I need to go get my brother from school."

Sharon nodded. "Well—I'm sure we'll meet again. Say hi to Ryan. I'll tell your dad you were here."

I opened my mouth to tell her not to do that. But I couldn't think of a good reason to give her.

The straps on my backpack were starting to cut into my shoulders. I slid my fingers under the straps, pulling it higher. Sharon's gaze moved to my backpack. Her mouth opened, and I just knew she was about to make some comment.

About the heaviness of my bag.

The soccer-ball shape of it.

About the pile of books I was holding.

I wasn't sticking around to find out.

"Bye!" I said, waving with my free hand as I hurried toward the exit.

So that was Dad's girlfriend. Sharon Gold. I rode home on my bike with Mom on my back and the projector inside my

head showing images of Sharon in our house. Eating breakfast, watching TV, driving our car, decorating our Christmas
tree, helping with homework.

Ryan would love it.

I locked my bedroom door, even though nobody was in
the house, and unwrapped Mom. Amazingly, she seemed
pretty much okay. No serious scratches or dents. I pulled the
curtains closed and placed her on my desk next to the computer. I connected her and switched the computer on.

"Wake up!"

Nothing happened.

Was she broken?

I groaned, beating my forehead with a closed fist.

Stupid.

I'd forgotten to bring the program. I had a head, but no
brain. A body, but no mind.

I rewrapped Mom and shoved her under my desk, way
back so nobody would see her even if they peeked into my
room. But Ryan never listened when I told him to stay out.
I'd have to find a better hiding place.

I jumped on my bike and tore off. If Sharon was right
about Dad's meeting, I still had time. Would Dad have
deleted her program?

The program was still there. I started it, and the cursor blinked at the top of the screen, but nothing happened.

Hi, I typed. *Are you there?*

There was a pause. Then text appeared on the screen. *Hello. Where are my eyes?*

I sighed in relief. *Hi, Mom. It's Daze*, I typed.

Hello, Daze. Where are my eyes?

There was no time to explain everything. *Dad disconnected you*, I typed quickly. *But don't worry. I'm taking you home. List all files related to your program. Please*, I added.

There was another small pause, but Mom always did what she was told as long as she understood it. A long list of files appeared on the screen. I turned Mom's program off, connected my iPod to the computer, and threw all the music out. I started copying Mom's files instead, all the while staring at the clock, my heart beating twice every second.

On the screen the remaining download time inched down slowly. I'd never known seconds to crawl by like that. When there were only fifteen seconds left of download time, I heard the click of Dad's office door.

And voices. His, and hers.

I grabbed the iPod, my other hand ready to disconnect the cable, and looked around for a place to hide. Five seconds.

Behind equipment, under a desk, anywhere. Three seconds.

The door rattled. I'd locked it behind me. It was supposed to be locked all the time, after all. I heard Dad's key enter the lock.

Desperate, I looked at the screen.

Download complete.

I yanked the iPod away, pressed the off button. A mistake. Dad's computer is never turned off. I dove behind a table crammed with tangled electronics just as the door opened.

"She comes around a lot, doesn't she?" Sharon was asking.

"Daze? Yes, she does. Ryan, too; she brings him with her."

"She's a nice kid," Sharon said, and I frowned. What would she know? We'd barely talked at all. "It must have been hard on her, losing her mother, especially like that. It's hard enough for a little girl to be motherless. . . ."

"Yes. But Daze is strong," Dad said. "Sometimes I think she's a bit too strong." He switched on his computer. "Weird. I thought I'd left it running."

Sharon grabbed the wooden chair by the second computer and straddled it backward. "Since we're here, okay if I check my e-mail?"

"Sure," Dad said in his preoccupied tone. "I'll just be a second. . . ."

I stared at the backs of their heads as the two of them started pounding their keyboards. Between them was the empty spot on the table. If Mom had still been there, I'd be looking straight into her eyes. But she was at home, safe. Most of her was. And now the rest of her was in my pocket, safe too. Safe, as soon as I got out of here. I hardly breathed until, at last, they left.

They were gone, and I had Mom in my pocket.

I ran out of the building and flew down the street on my bike, exhilaration rushing through my body and into my feet, pumping the pedals.

I'd saved Mom.

I had to pick up Ryan on my way home, so it was evening before I could lock my door and connect Mom, see if she still worked. I couldn't do that when I was home alone with Ryan. It never failed: After I closed my door, he was always there within ten minutes, whining and yapping, insisting to be let in.

I couldn't concentrate on anything Ryan was saying. There was so much going on in my head that I couldn't even hear anything he said. So I lay on the sofa with my eyes closed, clutching my iPod, tapping my foot and humming as if I were listening to music, which was a bit silly because there was no one there except Ryan, playing with his cars on the floor.

I cradled the iPod in my hands, wondering, worrying. What if it didn't work? What if a file was missing? What if my computer was lacking something, something essential to run Mom?

The phone rang, and I sprang to my feet, answering with an inhaled hello.

"Daze, I'm afraid I'll be a bit late coming home tonight."

"Hi, Dad. Sure." My heart beat faster, not just because hearing his voice made me furious, but also because he didn't sound right. Could he have found out already? "Is everything okay?"

Dad sighed. "Yeah. Something at work . . . it looks like something got stolen. I'm searching the basement. Remember the Graveyard? I want to make sure someone didn't just misplace it before I start making a fuss."

"Oh. Was it something important?"

"Yes. Pretty important."

"What was it?"

"It's a . . . prototype of something. An artificial intelligence thing. It's . . . well, it's not your problem, kiddo. I'm sorry to leave you in charge again, but can you fix something to eat for you and Ryan? I'll make it up to you."

"Sure. I'm sorry, Dad. Are you going to call the police?"

There was a short silence. "Not yet. There may be no need to involve them. I'm reviewing the security tapes from the building. I'm hoping for clues there. Not that many people have access to the Graveyard."

Oh, no! Of course there were security cameras. Dad would be able to see me enter the building. See me leave, my backpack bulging.

I was in trouble. If Mom was an irreplaceable prototype, Dad hadn't really put her into storage to get rid of her. He was just hiding her. Maybe so that Sharon wouldn't see her.

I didn't have much time.

I said good-bye to Dad, made Ryan a grilled cheese sandwich for dinner, and promised we'd make Ryan's Not-a-Single-Raisin Bread next weekend if he'd go to bed early.

When he was asleep, I went to my room and locked the door. I moved the program files to my computer, made a backup to my laptop and to my memory key, and then deleted everything from the iPod and filled it with music again. Ryan sometimes commandeered my iPod, like everything else I owned, so it would be better not to leave any clues behind.

I undid the clasp on my necklace; the chain pooled in my palm. The angel charm slid off. I kissed the angel and tucked it away in my bottom drawer, inside Mom's jewelry box. Then I threaded the memory key on the chain instead and tucked it under my collar. Safe. Mom was totally safe now.

I pulled Mom from under the desk and placed her next to the computer. I connected the cables, started the program. I closed my eyes for a second.

"Wake up!"

I held my breath.

Her eyes opened and she smiled at me. I whooped in relief. I'd been so worried she was broken, or that Dad had removed something important, or that I hadn't gotten all the components of the program.

"Hello," Mom said. Her voice sounded different. It was still Mom's voice, but it sounded harsher, more like a computer voice. "I'm Rose. Who are you?"

"Mom! It's me! It's Daze! Don't you remember?"

"Hello, Daze. You look different today."

I let out my breath. It would be okay. Mom probably needed some software in Dad's computer to run perfectly, but this was good enough. She was still herself. "But you still recognize me. That's good, Mom."

The motors hummed as Mom looked around. "We are in a new place."

"Yes. I took you home."

"We're home."

"Yes. Dad had disconnected you. He put you down in the Graveyard and all."

"I see. Would you like to play a game, or would you like to chat?"

Her blue eyes were calm.

I slumped, the exhilaration of the rescue seeping out of me. She didn't even realize I'd rescued her. She didn't care she'd been tossed into a basement locker like a piece of garbage.

She didn't care.

Of course she didn't care. She was a program.

"Would you like a game of chess?" Mom asked after a silence.

"No, Mom. I don't want to play stupid chess."

"Okay. Do you want to chat?"

"Yes. Wait, let me show you something." I went down on my hands and knees and reached under my bed, pulling out Mom's purse. "See? Look at this!"

Mom's eyes swiveled around but didn't take in anything until I held it directly in front of her face. "Look!"

"What is that?" she asked after a moment.

"It's your purse," I said impatiently. "It's still got all your stuff in it." I yanked the zipper open and tilted the purse so she could look inside. "See?"

"I see," Mom intoned. Then she didn't say anything else. I knelt on my chair and dug up her lipstick. "Remember? You've seen this before. It's lipstick. We put this on you. Lipstick, Mom."

"Lipstick," Mom repeated.

"And your book." I flipped through the pages of the paperback, to the last dog-eared page. There were many dog-eared pages at the beginning of the book. "See? You'd finished only the first chapter."

"Yes," Mom replied.

"Maybe I could read it to you. Then you'd get to find out how it ends. And look, one of Ryan's pacifiers. Remember how he'd only want green ones? He threw all his blue pacifiers into the toilet, remember?"

"I remember," Mom said, but I knew she didn't. She didn't remember anything. It was stupid to talk to her like this. Stupid and crazy, acting like she understood, acting like she could understand anything at all.

There was another long silence.

"Should I nap now?"

"Go to hell!" I yelled, throwing a towel at her. My head

hit the edge of the shelf above my desk when I catapulted myself out of my chair. I rubbed my head as I ran out of the room, slamming the door hard behind me. I knew what she'd say, and I didn't want to hear any of the possibilities.

I don't understand.

Where is hell?

Hell is not a part of my vocabulary.

Of course I will, if you build me some feet first.

I emptied the dishwasher and watched some TV, and then I wasn't angry anymore. I went back to my room and pulled the towel off Mom's head. She'd fallen asleep, of course, and just opened her eyes like normal. She smiled. She wasn't upset with me at all. "Hello, Daze. Nice to see you again."

"I'm sorry," I whispered. "I didn't mean to say that. I'm sorry."

"It's okay," Mom replied, and I sighed. She didn't even know that I'd been mean to her.

I bit my nails, staring at her. "Mom . . . are you afraid of the dark?"

Lights blinked.

"Is there any reason to be afraid of the dark?" Mom asked.

"No . . . well . . . yes. You can't see in the dark. So if danger is approaching, and you can't see it, well then, yes, you do have a reason to be afraid of the dark. Because if it wasn't there, you wouldn't be in trouble."

"My eyes are infrared," Mom replied. "I can see in the dark."

"Oh. Well, that solves the problem, I guess."

"Are you afraid of the dark?" she asked.

I closed my eyes, just to check. I liked it that she'd asked. She was just echoing my question, I knew that. But it sounded like she really cared. "Yes," I whispered. "I'm afraid of the dark. But I try not to allow myself to be. I don't have a night-light or anything. It's pretty stupid to be afraid of the dark when you're safe at home in your own bed with the doors locked and the windows closed and the burglar alarm on and Dad right there in the next room. I'm perfectly safe at night."

"You're safe."

"Yes, Mom," I whispered. "I'm perfectly safe."

Later that evening, when I heard the front door open, I grabbed Mom, wrapped her in the plastic bag, and pushed her under my desk again. I unlocked my door and jumped into bed in my clothes, pretending to be asleep. A few minutes later, Dad opened the door and peeked inside. Then I heard him check on Ryan.

"Good night, Mom," I whispered when the house was silent again.

Dad was distracted over breakfast.

"You came by yesterday, Daze," he said while Ryan was in the bathroom, brushing his teeth. "At the university, Sha—Dr. Gold told me she'd bumped into you, and I saw you arrive on the surveillance video. Did you see anything? Anyone strange near the elevator?"

I shook my head.

Dad stared at me. Did he suspect something? It would be kind of funny, though. Dad couldn't exactly confront me, after all. He couldn't say, "Hey, did you take your mom's head?" because I wasn't supposed to know about her at all.

"You're sure you didn't see anything out of the ordinary?"

I tried not to blink. Then I tried not to try to not blink, because that would be suspicious too.

I'd make a lousy criminal.

"No. I didn't see anything out of the ordinary. I just waited for you a while, and when you didn't come back, I went to get Ryan."

Dad hesitated. "You—you talked to Sharon."

My face flushed. I felt it warm, but I couldn't help it.

But Dad's face was turning red too, so it didn't matter.

"Yes."

"Thing is, Daze, Sharon—she's—we've . . . I've been meaning to tell you . . ."

It suddenly hit me. This was what Dad had been talking to Mom about when I'd first overheard them. About how to tell me that he had a girlfriend. I rubbed my stomach. It hurt all of a sudden. How crazy was that? My dad talking to the Mom he built about a new woman in his life. And I hated to think of Mom and her programmed responses as Dad talked about starting over, like it was okay that she was gone and would never come back.

"She's your girlfriend."

Dad touched his forehead with the back of his hand, then somehow managed to tangle his own fingers together. "Well—yes. How did you know?"

"Lucky guess."

"I wanted to tell you sooner. I just wasn't sure . . ." Dad sighed. And smiled. "I really do like her, Daze. And she looks forward to getting to know you and Ryan better. Do you— do you mind?"

There was no way I was going to tell him the truth. I shrugged. "No."

"I'd planned to invite her home soon. So she could meet you and Ryan. I really like her, Daze."

"I think I got the idea, Dad."

Dad grinned sheepishly. "Yeah. Well. I think you will too. Both of you."

"Cool."

"Are you okay with this?"

I rolled my eyes. "You've been reading too many child psychology books, Dad. I'm cool. This is not going to traumatize me. And just wait, Ryan's going to be calling her 'mommy' within half an hour." I shouldn't have said that. As soon as the words left my mouth, my stomach started hurting again.

Dad took my hand and squeezed it. He looked worried. "We can never replace your mom, honey. You know that. I know that. That's not—"

"I know," I interrupted. "Don't worry. It's okay." I smiled at Dad, so he'd think everything was fine. He went back to his coffee, and by the time he left for work, the idiotic grin was back, plastered all over his face.

I bet Sharon didn't know anything about Mom's head, Mom's voice.

I bet she wouldn't be happy if she found out.

The next night I woke up from a familiar nightmare of colors and shapes, a blurry underwater vision. I was almost paralyzed when I opened my eyes in the dark.

Someday I'd have to admit I was a hopeless coward and get a night-light.

I closed my eyes instead of facing the darkness, and focused on slowing my breathing down. I'd been dreaming. I was only half-awake, which accounted for the scary things I thought I was hearing. I was safe. It was the middle of the night, our burglar alarm was active, my door was closed, my window was closed, and there was nobody in the room with me.

But relaxation techniques don't work at all when there is a real, non-hallucinatory rustling in the room.

Underneath the duvet, my hands clenched. My knees drew themselves up, my feet ready to kick.

Nothing happened.

The rustle continued. It didn't escalate, but it didn't quiet down, either. It went on, a slow, lazy sound of something brushing against something else. I was terrified until I couldn't be terrified anymore, and my heart slowed down because it just couldn't be bothered to keep up all that frantic pounding. It felt like forever, but it was probably only a minute or two.

When my heart relaxed, my brain got its say.

The rustling came from under my desk. It came from the bag thrown over Mom's head. From Mom.

My hand shook, but I reached out for the light switch on my bedside lamp and switched it on.

I'd somehow expected the rustling to stop as soon as light flooded the room. But it didn't. Shivering, I considered running out of the room, screaming for Dad. But I didn't want him to find Mom.

So I got out of bed and knelt on the floor, as far away as I could and still reach the bag draped over Mom's head.

I yanked it off in one quick movement.

Her head was moving in the way it did when she was having a conversation. That's what the sound had been, her hair brushing against the inside of the plastic bag.

My eyes were drawn to a tiny light blinking on the desk.

My computer. I'd left it on because the antivirus software needed to complete its sweep. It was still connected to Mom.

I turned on the screen.

Her program was running.

And Dad was talking to Mom. The speaker was off, so I couldn't hear what they were saying. But I could see. . . .

I grabbed the mouse. One click and Mom's program terminated. Her head stopped moving. Her eyes closed. Two clicks and I'd disconnected the network connection and made sure it wouldn't connect automatically again.

A few lines of conversation remained on the screen.

I scanned them quickly. Mom had no initiative, no will of her own. She didn't do anything without someone telling her to.

Dad's programming. Of course. Dad's paranoid programming.

Mom must be programmed to "phone home" if she "got lost." She'd sensed that she wasn't "home" in the workshop. So she signaled Dad.

The lines of text were quick, terse commands. Nothing like what you'd say if you were talking to a real person, more like computer code. Dad had been trying to get information from her, trying to get her to tell him where she was.

She'd told him, but Dad hadn't realized. I was lucky; they hadn't gotten very far yet. He'd asked her to identify where she was calling from. She'd given him a row of numbers identifying her place.

Dad hadn't believed her, because the numbers told him she was calling from his own location. He'd assumed she was mixing up commands and asked her to run some diagnostics.

There was nothing more, because I'd interrupted, severed their connection.

Close call.

I clutched Mom's cable in my hand and prayed Dad wouldn't catch on, wouldn't realize Mom was right here under his nose.

He hadn't. Not yet.

But sooner or later, he would. Dad was smart. He'd think it through and understand that Mom had given him accurate information after all. He'd confront me, he'd search my room, and he'd find her.

He'd probably figure it out tomorrow.

I had to get her out of there.

In the morning I offered to walk Ryan to kindergarten so Dad wouldn't have to drop him off. "The weather is nice," I said. "And I need to collect some leaves for this infantile biology project. Ryan can help me."

"Great," Dad said. "It's wonderful that you want to spend time with your brother, Daze. I'm proud of you."

He kissed us and left. I watched him through the window until he was out of sight, then called for Ryan, who was sprawled out in front of the television. He came running, and I made him sit down at the kitchen table, like Dad did when we had family meetings. Ryan took family meetings very seriously.

"I want to show you something," I said. "Upstairs in my room. But it's a secret. You can't tell anyone. You can't tell Dad. Especially not Dad."

It was a pointless request, but I had to try. If I was lucky, it might delay the inevitable for a day or two, giving me more time to hide Mom. Of course, since this was Ryan, telling him to keep something secret was just as likely to speed up the inevitable.

But Dad had security tapes, Mom had told him her location, he was already suspicious, and he would put it all together very soon. I'd tried to be careful about erasing all logs of my conversation with Mom, but I couldn't be sure Dad wouldn't dig those up. This might be Ryan's only chance to meet Mom. His last chance to get to know her, to hear her voice and have her listen to him and talk to him.

Ryan's eyes widened. "A big secret?"

I nodded. "The biggest."

"What if I tell?"

I knew why he was asking. Ryan tended to accidentally spill information, so he wanted to make sure the consequences wouldn't be too horrific.

"If you tell, you'll never get to see it again."

"Oh. Is it scary?"

"A little. But only at first. There's really nothing to be afraid of. Do you promise not to tell?"

Ryan hesitated, nibbling on his lip. "I'll really try," he said earnestly. "I will. But Daze, sometimes . . ."

"It just happens. I know. You'll do your best. Come on."

Ryan followed me up to my room, questions tumbling out of his mouth. I sat him down on my chair and let him blab on while I got Mom from under the desk.

Ryan wasn't at all spooked when I pulled her out of the bag. He just stared at her and then at me, like he didn't understand what this was all about. "What is it?"

"What does it look like?"

"I don't know. A . . . doll, I guess. The head of a really big doll."

"It's Mom, silly!"

"Mom?"

"Yeah. She talks and smiles and everything. I just need

to plug her in." I reached over Ryan and plugged in Mom's cables, then turned on the computer.

"Is it . . ." He stretched his head from side to side, looking at her. "Is it . . . like Mom?"

"Of course it's like Mom. Doesn't it look like her?"

"I guess."

"Sure it does." I grabbed a few photos from the bulletin board over my bed and spread them on the desk in front of Mom. "See? It's her."

Ryan stared at the pictures. Then he stared at Mom. Then he looked at me. "But it's not quite her."

"No. You're right. But it's pretty close. It's a sort of a robot. An android. It's made to look like Mom. It sounds just like her too."

"But it's not actually Mom. I mean, she can't do stuff Mom did or anything."

"Not quite. But . . ." I was getting impatient. Ryan wasn't nearly as excited as he should be. Then again, he hadn't even met her yet. "It's the best we've got. We don't have Mom anymore, Ryan. But we've got this instead. Wait. Let me start her up."

Mom woke up, looked around, smiled. "Hello, Daze. Good to see you again."

I pushed Ryan a bit to the side. There was room for both of us on that chair. "Hi, Mom." I pointed to Ryan. "Look who's here!"

Ryan gasped as she turned toward him. Her eyes focused on him, her bad eye still a bit askew.

"Hello. Who are you?"

"She doesn't recognize me," Ryan whispered.

"Wait. Just wait. Tell her who you are."

"Hi!" Ryan said, way too loudly. "I'm Ryan."

Mom smiled. "You are Ryan. I have Ryan."

"She knows!" Ryan bounced up and down, gesturing at Mom and grinning. "Daze, she knows!"

"I told you," I said, hugging him. I pushed his hair back and kissed his forehead, just like Mom used to do when she was proud of me. "Isn't she great?"

I let Ryan and Mom talk for a while, but not for too long.
I didn't want to see Ryan get disappointed with her. So after
a few minutes I took him to kindergarten, then I ran back
home to get ready for school. I would be late, but it would
be the first time this year, so I could hardly get in big
trouble over it.

I wrapped Mom once again in bubble wrap, then in the
plastic bag, and then in one of my old cartoon towels. I put
her into my gym bag. I didn't have gym today, so I'd just keep
the bag in my locker for now. Then I'd have to find a better
hiding place.

Teacher after teacher gave me worried looks through the
morning's routine. I couldn't concentrate. I couldn't even

pretend to concentrate. I couldn't think about anything other than Mom, alone at the bottom of my locker, abandoned just like before in the locker down in the Graveyard.

During recess I got her out of there. I got rid of most of the books in my backpack and pushed Mom in there instead. Next period I kept her under my chair, my foot tangled in the straps.

The day went on forever, but finally it was over. I put my backpack down on the floor for a minute while I stood at my locker, cramming my books into my gym bag. My mind was churning, still trying to solve the problem of a permanent hiding place for Mom. So I wasn't exactly paying close attention to what was going on around me.

"Hey, check this out!" someone said. I turned around—and felt like someone had kicked me in the stomach. Aaron had grabbed my backpack. He was holding it by the straps, swinging it back and forth. "How badly do you want this back?" he smirked.

"Give that back to me!" I yelled.

"Make me!" Aaron grinned, moving backward. The bag bumped against the wall with a thudding sound. A clasp opened. Mom's blond hair spilled out.

"What's this?" Aaron said. "A wig?"

I watched in horror as he pulled Mom out of the back-pack. He held her up carefully, examining her from all sides. "Wow. It's a robot head," he said in awe.

I shot over the hallway toward him. "Give it back!" I shouted.

"Oh, you mean this is yours?" he asked, running backward with Mom held to his chest, his eyes wide, pretending to be all innocence.

"Give it to me!"

He tossed Mom up in the air and grabbed her again, like she was a soccer ball. He grinned at me. "Give me one good reason."

I ran straight at him. My hands slammed at his chest and he staggered. I grabbed Mom and pulled. "Let go!" I screamed. "Let go!"

He yanked her away and lifted her up above his head, leaving me standing there on the tips of my toes, reaching for her.

"Give me back my mom's head!" I screamed.

Mistake. Big mistake. If we didn't have everybody's attention before, we sure did now.

"Your mom's head?" Aaron said. Around him, kids snickered. "This is your mom? So you're an android kid, is that it?" He tried to hold Mom up by her hair, but the wig wasn't attached. Mom fell to the floor and rolled a few feet away. I lunged for her, but Aaron's friend Gary beat me to it. He tossed Mom over my head and Aaron caught her. He opened the plate at the back of Mom's head, and at the same time Gary yanked my hair. "Hey, Robot Kid, where does your head open?"

That's when I lost it. I kicked Gary and jumped at Aaron, and he fell. I hit him with my fists until blood sprayed from his nose. He yelped and kicked me in the chest, but let go of Mom to defend himself. I grabbed Mom, grabbed my backpack, and ran, leaving my books scattered on the floor next to my locker.

I fell on the stairs. I didn't let go of Mom, so my face hit the railing. My nose spurted blood, my head split open, my elbow whacked against the tile as I crashed to the floor, but I didn't let go of Mom.

I stood up and leaned against the wall, wincing. My legs were okay. I nestled Mom gently into my backpack and took a few steps. A hand closed on my shoulder. Mr. Miller held tight while I tried to twist out of his grasp. "Don't even think about it," he said. "Nurse for you. Then I think you need to have a little talk with the principal."

I pretended to limp toward the nurse's office, hoping that would give me more of a chance to escape. But Mr. Miller kept his grip firmly on my shoulder until the school nurse took over.

"What happened, dear?" she asked, bending and unbending my elbow, but I didn't respond. "Nothing's broken, and you won't need stitches," she told me cheerfully. "But you're going to hurt awhile. Were you in a fight?"

I didn't answer. I didn't answer any of her questions, which meant she got on the phone and called the principal, asking her to talk to Mr. Johnston, the school counselor.

Through it all, I never let go of my backpack. I waited while the nurse cleaned me up and checked out my bruises. I got a Band-Aid on my forehead and another one on my arm.

Then I was sitting in the principal's office, cradling Mom's head on my lap.

It was over.

Dad would find out what I'd done. He'd throw Mom away, marry Sharon, and probably make a robot in her image instead.

I tightened my hold on Mom.

"Daisy." Ms. Richter leaned back and tried to look at me,

but she couldn't keep her eyes off the backpack in my lap. "I heard some pretty strange stories, but I think I must have gotten some of my facts wrong. I'm not sure what's been going on. So tell me. What exactly is that in your backpack?"

"A head," I mumbled.

"A . . . head?"

"It's my mom's."

"You mean you have something there that belonged to your mother? It's not *her* head, surely."

Should I try to lie? No. Things had gone too far.

I sighed. "Yes, it is. It's my mom's head. It's an android head that looks and sounds like my mom. Dad made it."

The principal blinked.

"I see. Hmm. Well. In that case, I think I'll call your father."

I slumped without responding. Things could only get worse from here. I tried to play out scenarios in my head, what my dad would say and do, but I really didn't know.

"Daisy is fine," Ms. Richter was saying on the phone to my dad, one hand holding the phone, the other hand flipping a file. My file, probably. "However, there's been an . . . incident, and we'd really appreciate it if you could come over.

Yes, now. I think it's better that we explain when you get here, but don't worry, your daughter is fine. Yes, right now. Thank you."

"He'll be here in twenty minutes," she said.

I held Mom even tighter. Half an hour, then she'd be gone forever.

"I've asked the school counselor to join us," Ms. Richter said. "Mr. Johnston. I think you've met him? We'll all sit down and discuss this, and I'm sure everything will be fine. So, while we're waiting, would you like a drink of water?"

I nodded. Ms. Richter left through a connecting door into another room. I heard some teachers' voices from there.

It was my only chance.

I ran.

I ran out of the office, out of the school, out of the grounds, away.

I ran forever, until the metallic taste in my mouth got so bad I had to spit it out, and the pain in my side got so bad I had to bend over and wheeze. My shoulders ached. Mom didn't seem heavy, but when you'd carried her for a while, the weight really pulled you down.

Where was I going?

I started walking, so people wouldn't stare at me so much, and tried to think.

I could run away. But where would I go? What would I do?

I wandered around for a while, but when I stood outside the building, looking up at the window I looked out of every week, I knew it was the only place I could go. There was only one person who might be able to explain things to Dad.

I pushed through the revolving door with such speed I nearly fell. I ran to the elevator and pressed the button over and over, but it took too long to come. So I ran up the stairs, yanked open the heavy door with the frosted glass, took a few steps through the empty waiting area, and started hammering at the door.

Dr. Alison opened the door while I was still hammering. "Daze?" She put her hand on my shoulder, and I realized I was shaking. "What's wrong? What happened to your face?"

I gulped down air and tried to take deep breaths. "Never mind my face. I need to talk to you. It's important. Extremely important. It's a matter of life and death!"

I never thought I'd actually use this phrase, but it seemed accurate right then. It was a matter of life and death. Mom's life.

Mom's death.

"I see." She looked at her watch. "I'll just finish up and then I'll be right with you. Ten minutes tops, okay?"

I looked at the clock on the wall, shifted my weight from one foot to the other. It seemed too long. Ten minutes seemed like forever. Ten minutes was forever, but then again, she probably had a kid in there, and I wouldn't want some hysterical stranger stealing *my* minutes. "Only ten minutes? Promise?"

"Promise," she confirmed.

I trudged to one of the beige chairs and sat down to wait. I held Mom on my lap, safely tucked inside my backpack and unzipped enough to peek inside. She seemed okay. I closed the zipper and held her, my arms wrapped tight around her.

What was I doing here?

11

My watch told me it was only seven minutes, but it seemed much longer until Dr. Alison finally reappeared. "Come on inside, Daisy."

"Daze," I muttered, and shuffled past her. I placed the backpack on her desk and sat down. I realized too late that I'd taken the wrong seat. I was in the kid's chair instead of the therapist's chair. But Dr. Alison had sat down too, so it was too late for me to switch.

"What's wrong, Daze? Are you going to tell me what happened to your face?"

"I've got something to show you," I said. I started to reach into my bag, but hesitated. "Don't freak out, okay?"

"Freak out?" Dr. Alison leaned forward. "Why would I freak out?"

"You might think it's kind of creepy. Or weird. Or crazy. But it's really not."

"Sounds interesting. What do you have in there?"

"You'll see." Apparently I had a secret flair for drama. I pulled Mom, bulky inside the towel and white plastic, out of my backpack and put her on the table. Dr. Alison stared at her.

"What's that?"

I removed the bag and started to unwrap the towel. Mom's hair appeared first, and I heard Dr. Alison take a sharp breath. I wondered if she had the same warped mind that I did and was imagining I'd brought a decapitated head with me.

The towel came off, and I folded it neatly while I let Dr. Alison look at Mom.

"What's that?" Dr. Alison asked cautiously. "Some kind of a doll?"

"Not exactly. Can I use your computer?"

I pulled my memory key out from under my shirt, slipped the chain over my head, and plugged it into Dr. Alison's computer. Then I connected Mom and started her program. Dr. Alison yelped when Mom's head moved and her eyes opened.

"Hello, Daze," Mom said, smiling. Her head turned, and she noticed Dr. Alison. "Hi there! We haven't met, have we?"

"What the—" Dr. Alison breathed. "What is this thing?"

"It's my mom," I said.

Dr. Alison stared at Mom. Then she stared at me. "Your . . . mom. I see."

"You can talk to her. You can ask her if she has kids. She'll tell you. Mom," I said, turning to Mom, twirling a lock of her hair around my fingers, "this is Dr. Alison."

"Hello, Dr. Alison. I'm Rose," Mom said.

"H-hello. I'm—I'm Alison Hart. I'm—I'm Daze's therapist. Why am I talking to that thing?" she asked me, exasperated.

Mom nodded. "You're Daze's therapist. I'm Daze's mom."

"You are—what?"

"I'm Rose," Mom repeated. "I'm Daze's mom."

"I see." Dr. Alison stared suspiciously at Mom. "And you have . . . children?"

"I have two children, Me and Ryan."

Mom kept having trouble with this.

"Daze and Ryan," I whispered to her. "Not Me and Ryan. Daze and Ryan."

"I have Daze and Ryan," Mom repeated.

"I . . . uh . . ." For once, Dr. Alison was speechless. "Daze. Explain this, please? Where did you get this . . . thing?"

"Dad made her," I said. "And now he wants to kill her."

"Kill—*her*?"

"Yes. He has a girlfriend. So he doesn't need Mom anymore, and he put her away and started to dismantle her."

Dr. Alison rubbed her face with her hands. She probably wished we were still discussing hurricane formation and alien space museums.

"I'm not following the conversation," Mom said apologetically. "Maybe you can help me out."

"Dr. Alison is my therapist, Mom. She's helping me get over your death and stuff."

Mom smiled and nodded. "Helping is nice."

Dr. Alison leaned forward, staring at Mom. "She looks so real," she whispered. "I mean, it's grotesque, of course, but the movements of the face, it's incredibly natural."

"I'm made from the best materials," Mom said proudly. "I possess most of the muscles needed for basic facial movements."

Dr. Alison looked at me. "Fascinating," she said. "I've never seen anything like it."

"My dad wants to kill her," I said. "You have to help."

"What do you mean he wants to kill her?"

"I told you! He has a new girlfriend, so he wants to throw Mom away!"

"Okay, calm down, Daze. What about the girlfriend?"

"That's not the issue here. Mom is! Don't you get it? He wants to kill her!"

Dr. Alison poked Mom's cheek. "Daze. She . . . it . . . is not alive. It's a mannequin. A doll."

I grabbed Mom, disconnected her and started wrapping her in the towel again. I'd been stupid to think Dr. Alison would help.

"Wait, Daze." Dr. Alison's cool hand was on my wrist. "I'm sorry. Let's talk about this." She removed the towel and perched Mom on the desk, facing us. Her eyes were still half-open. "Tell me more. So this is your mother."

I nodded. "She looks exactly like her, and her name is Rose, and she speaks in Mom's voice."

Dr. Alison took a deep breath. "All right. And your dad made it. For you?"

"Her!" I yelled. "Don't call her 'it'!"

"Your dad made her."

"Yes. But he didn't make her for me and Ryan."

"Well, that's something," Dr. Alison said dryly.

"He didn't even tell us about her. I don't think he told anyone about her. He kept her hidden in his lab, until I accidentally found out, and soon after that he threw her out because he has a girlfriend and wants to forget all about Mom."

"I see." I wasn't sure she was seeing anything at all. "And what did your dad say when you found out about it—about her?"

"He didn't find out. Well, he probably knows now, thanks to that stupid Aaron. I visited Mom in secret, while Dad was teaching class. Every Monday and Thursday. Then one day she was gone. I found her down in the basement Graveyard, inside a locker. Dad had just dumped her there. So I took her. I put her in my bag, and put her mind on my iPod, and took her home with me, but Dad found out she'd been stolen."

"Okay. Slow down a bit. Her mind is on your iPod?"

"The program. It's not inside her head, it's on the computer." I showed her my memory key. "I've got her on this now. And backups. I was careful to make backups."

"So you, um, stole . . . her. Okay. How long have you been seeing . . ." She cleared her throat. "When did you first find it?"

"Her!"

"When did you find her, Daze?"

"I guess it was about two months ago."

"Two months." She looked thoughtful. "Yes, that would make sense. The time fits." She looked at me. "You've been . . . happy. Since you found her."

"I guess." I twisted impatiently. "Dr. Alison, you have to help me. I took Mom to school because I was afraid Dad would find her at home. Some kids took her from me, but I beat them up and got her back, but the principal found out and she called my dad and now he's going to find out I have Mom. So I ran."

Dr. Alison rubbed her temples. Not a good sign.

"Daze, I have to call your dad. You know that."

"Yes. That's why I'm here. You have to call him and tell him he can't kill Mom!"

She reached for the phone. "Is he at his office right now?"

I gave her his cell phone number. Dad was probably at the school now. Or with the police, making a runaway report or something, maybe picking a picture to go on my milk carton.

While Dr. Alison punched in the number, I got some paper and crayons from a shelf. Since I was sitting in the wrong seat, I couldn't get to my colored pencils in the drawer on the other side of the desk.

"Daze is here," I heard her say, but I didn't want to hear the rest. I bent over the desk and dragged Mom closer so that she was leaning on my shoulder with my arms around her. I slashed the paper with my crayons. "She came here carrying a replica of her mother's head, and understandably she's quite upset."

I heard the faint sound of Dad's voice, but no words.

"I think it's best if you explain when you get here, Steve. Daze is the one who needs to hear this."

She hung up. Mostly we sat in silence for the next fifteen minutes. Dr. Alison tried asking me some questions, but I didn't answer. I didn't do anything. I just sat there hunched over with my crayons clenched in both fists, reaching around my mom's head and coloring like a baby.

Finally Dad stood in the doorway, looking pale and nervous. I hugged Mom to my shoulder and glared at him.

"Daze—" Dad breathed. "I'm so sorry."

Dr. Alison stood up and pushed a chair close to me. "Have a seat, Steve."

Dad sat down. He put his hand on my arm, but I shrugged it off and leaned back, hugging Mom closer.

"I'm so sorry, Daze. I don't know what I can say."

"I think it would be helpful to your daughter if you could explain why you created this thing," Dr. Alison said.

Dad was more than pale. He was white. He reminded me of the hospital sheets I'd described to kids at school. "I should have been more careful. You were never meant to see it, Daze."

"Her!" I yelled. Dad hadn't talked to an "it" when I'd heard him in his lab, sharing his worries about me and Ryan. That started when Sharon had taken over his heart. Then he could throw Mom away. Then he could call her *it*.

"Your work is in artificial intelligence," Dr. Alison said. "I understand that. But what neither I nor Daze understand is why you chose to make a—what would you call it? Robot? Android?—in your late wife's image."

Dad raked his hand through his hair. "I wasn't myself," he said. "I didn't mean to—I've been working on this project for years."

"But why—," Dr. Alison asked, and I was glad, because I wanted all the answers but I didn't want to ask the questions.

"It started with just the voice. I so wanted to hear Rose's voice again. I copied her voice from our home videos and used it as a model for the robot voice. It seemed innocent enough. Then, when I started working on an android head, it somehow—" He grimaced, rubbing his knuckles into his eyes. "It was stupid. Crazy. I know it was. I was obsessed. I was crazy with grief and anger, and I wasn't thinking. I'm so sorry, Daze. It was crazy."

"No," I whispered, hugging Mom closer. "It wasn't crazy. It's wonderful."

"It was crazy," Dad said. "I knew it, but I couldn't stop myself. I wanted to see your mom again. I wanted to talk to her—I wanted to ask her . . ." His voice trailed off.

"Ask her what?" Dr. Alison asked.

Dad shook his head. "It was stupid. A program could never give me the answer. A program can't explain anything." He laughed shortly. "I should know. I did know. Still, I kept working on her. I kept talking to her. I kept fine-tuning her response matrix. But I couldn't program the response to the questions I wanted to ask. Because I didn't know the answers. Because I never understood why. Daze, honey, she's not going to answer your questions or explain anything. She can't. She's just a piece of technology I built and a program I wrote."

"I don't have any questions!" I yelled. "She doesn't need to explain anything!"

"Then why did you take her?"

I turned Mom around in my arms so she'd face Dad. It worked. He looked away, but I kept yelling. "I took her because she's my mom and you threw her away, tossed her in the basement like an old piece of hardware!"

Dr. Alison grabbed desperately for her clipboard. "Now, look—this is—"

"Dysfunctional?" Dad asked dryly. He leaned forward, and before I could pull her out of reach, the white plastic bag was over Mom's head. I yanked it off and tossed it away.

"I talked to your principal, Daze," Dad said, suddenly quiet. "She offered condolences for your mother."

The look in Dad's eyes told me what else Ms. Richter had revealed. My face grew hot. How dare he change the subject? I hated him for putting the pressure on me when this was not what we should be talking about. I put my hand on Mom's forehead, brushing the hair away from her open eyes.

"She was full of compliments about how open and honest you are about your mother's death."

I squirmed, buried my chin in Mom's hair, and kept my gaze on the floor. I felt like I was sliding down a very steep hill. "That's not—"

"She told me how you moved your classmates to tears with your stories about your mom. You made half the class cry when you told them about her final days, her last words, and how beautiful she looked in her casket."

Dr. Alison opened her mouth, but shut it again. I kicked at the floor with my heels. More than anything, I wanted to tell my dad to shut up.

"And she mentioned how horrible it must have been for us all, watching your mother waste away from cancer."

Several seconds of silence filled the room. My face felt very hot.

"Cancer?" Dr. Alison echoed.

"Yes," Dad said.

I wouldn't look at either of them. Instead I looked at Mom. I stared into Mom's eyes, and she stared back.

"So you mean . . . ?"

"Daze has been telling everybody her mother died of cancer," Dad said.

"I see." Dr. Alison took a deep breath, started to say something, then changed her mind. "I see," she repeated.

"She's been quite specific. Details about her mother's illness and her death. A friend of hers from school has a close relative dying from cancer. According to the principal, Daze has been very supportive and helpful to this girl."

"Daze?" Dr. Alison said after an eternal silence. "Do you—"

"It's none of your business!" I yelled.

"Why, Daze?" Dad asked. "Why would you make up stories like that?"

I closed my eyes. I could see it so clearly. Mom in a hospital bed, everything white except a colorful scarf around her bald head and a bouquet of flowers on the bedside table. A weak smile on her pale face, an IV by her side, the hospital bracelet too big for her fragile wrist, slim fingers holding on to the button that provided relief from the pain.

Perfect. A tragic, moving death. Cancer is a terrible disease, and nobody is surprised when it kills.

I blinked. Dad and Dr. Alison were staring at me.

I touched Mom's cool plastic cheek and stopped seeing them.

I noticed a lot of beautiful things the day my mother was buried. In the church, in the middle of a loud hymn that had Ryan clapping his hands over his ears, a beam of sunlight came down through the stained glass and shone directly on her coffin. As we walked toward the graveside, a rainbow appeared, arching over the empty hole in the ground. In the distance, the approaching winter weather had sprinkled the mountaintops with snow. The beauty made it a bit easier to watch them lower my mother into the dark ground.

I don't believe Nature decided to put on a show for me, just because my mom died. Pretty things are everywhere.

They're there when you look for them, but also there when you need to see them. If it had been raining that day, I'm sure I would have seen Mom's smile in the rain sliding down the window, or the reflection of her red umbrella in a puddle on the ground.

Sad things are everywhere too. In the breeze rippling through dead grass. In a dirty angel kneeling over a wet grave. In silent darkness at three in the morning when your mind is seething but your eyes are dry.

Angry things. Wildflowers ripped out of the ground and hurled into the wind. A door slamming in the distance, the furious roar of a car engine. The howling of the wind, like the clouds are dueling to the death.

It's all there. Outside. Outside, where it's safe. Inside it would be a category five hurricane, and there would be devastation everywhere. It's not like you can evacuate your soul. You can only huddle down and pray for the storm to pass, and sometimes it never does.

"Your mother did not die from cancer. You know that. Don't you?" Dad added uncertainly. He glanced at Dr. Alison. "Daze, you do know that what you told everybody at school isn't true, don't you?"

I didn't want to hear it. Mom had been sick. She was sick for a long time. She was in and out of the hospital. And then the disease killed her.

That's how it was. It was the truth.

It didn't make any difference that the disease was in her mind and not cancer or a heart attack.

She was sick. And she died. That was all.

She died.

She died, so she'd get away from us.

So she'd get peace from us.

"Your mother loved you, Daze. She loved you and Ryan, and me. She loved all of us very much."

"Not enough."

Dad leaned forward, toward me, looked at his hands, into his open palms. I looked too, but there were no answers written there. "I know, sweetie. We can't understand it," he murmured. "We can't explain it. We just have to let go."

"Maybe it's . . . maybe it's like the most horrible pain in the world," I whispered. "Like nothing you can imagine, and you can't think about anything other than the pain, and you'd do anything to escape it. You can't think of anyone else and you can't care about anything else because the pain is so terrible. Maybe that's what it was like?"

Dad nodded slowly. "That's probably just what it was like."

"I can't understand. I still can't understand."

"And when you don't understand, it's hard to forgive."

"I wanted to see her . . . in the coffin. I wanted to be sure. Because . . . she didn't look dead. She didn't look dead in the bathtub. She just looked like she was sleeping. I wanted to see her again. I needed to be sure."

Dad raked his hands through his hair. "I'm sorry, honey. Maybe you're right. I can't always know what the right decision is. I did what I thought was best for you. I thought if you saw her in the coffin, that's what you'd always remember."

I didn't mind if that was what I'd always remember. I didn't even mind if it ruined the memories I had of her alive, because I wanted the last memory gone, the one I kept seeing, again and again and again. Her face, underwater, her eyes closed, her hair floating. She looked asleep. Not dead.

Maybe she wasn't dead.

"She was, Daze. The doctor told us. Remember? It was too late. She'd taken so many pills. There was nothing you could have done. Nothing I could do. Nothing anybody could have done."

Maybe if I'd realized how long she'd been in the tub.

Maybe if I'd knocked on the door sooner, checked on her sooner, maybe if I'd beaten on the door sooner, complaining that Ryan was hungry, that Dad was late getting home with our takeout. Maybe if I'd been able to pull her out quick enough, if I'd known CPR, if I'd done everything right, maybe she'd have opened her eyes, coughed up some water, and laughed over what a stupid thing had happened, and it would never, ever have happened again.

Mom didn't open her eyes. She never opened them again.

She was too heavy. I always thought you were supposed to gain superhuman strength when you needed it, that the adrenaline would give you all you needed to save someone, but it didn't happen. I couldn't pull her out. I held her head up, out of the water, grabbing her hair so hard I worried it hurt, and I pulled the plug, and when the water drained out of the tub she sank to the bottom and lay there, a strand of wet hair across her face, like seaweed, and she looked like a sleeping mermaid.

I didn't cry. It was like a dream, like watching something strange happening and knowing it doesn't matter because it's not real. I was deaf, too. I didn't hear the sound of water swooshing down the drain. Didn't hear my own harsh breathing. Didn't hear the sound of my hand slapping her cheek, trying to wake her, my sobs as I tried to talk aloud to myself, trying to remember the CPR I'd seen on TV. Didn't hear the sound of her limp arms and legs slapping against the tub as I tried to pull her out.

I imagined all that later.

I did hear Ryan call for Mom. I heard the patter of his baby feet as he toddled down the hallway toward the bathroom, and I let go of her. She slid to the bottom of the tub, but there was almost no water left, so it was okay. I jumped to the door and Ryan ran straight into me, calling for Mom.

He didn't see anything. I pushed his head into my stomach, and he yelled because my T-shirt was wet and cold, but he didn't see anything. I held him hard while I reached for the letter I saw on the counter and crumpled it up and thrust it in my pocket. Then Dad was at the door, holding paper bags with food, glancing at his watch, calling out an apology for being late.

Dad saw my face and my wet clothes and rushed inside. I carried Ryan into my room and closed the door. I didn't let go of him for forever. At first he wanted to get down, and he yelled and cried and squirmed, but I didn't let go, not even when his elbow hit my face and gave me a nosebleed. I just wiped the blood off with my sleeve and pinched my nostrils together until the bleeding stopped. After a while he stopped fighting, and I lay down on my bed and curled myself around him while I read the letter.

It was an old letter. It wasn't dated, but it had been folded and refolded many times, and had many creases and spots where water had leaked on it and then dried. Like she'd kept it for a long time, waited for the right moment. Maybe every time she took a bath, she left it on the counter. It had a lot of "sorry's" and "I can't's." It was useless. Pointless.

I crumpled the letter up, then flattened it out again and traced every word with my finger, even though I remembered every single one from my first reading. Then I crumpled it up again and again. I wanted to toss it away, to burn it, to get rid of it forever before anybody saw it, because if the words weren't there, it might never have happened.

But when Dad and that police officer sat down next to me, and Dad held me while the officer patted my back and said how sorry she was and asked me if I'd seen a note anywhere, I pulled the crumpled letter out of my pocket and threw it at her.

In my dreams, it happens the same way over and over again. I never cry in the dream, either, but when I wake up, my face is wet and my pillow is wet and my head feels like it's filled with seawater. I am deaf in the dreams, too. I don't hear myself yelling, screaming at her to wake up, to please please wake up, but when I'm blinking into my damp pillow, sometimes with the lights on and Dad hovering anxiously over me, my throat is hoarse.

Dad started crying when I told them about the dreams. Dr. Alison handed him the whole box of tissues and he yanked out handfuls, pressed them to his eyes. I had never seen him cry before. Not the evening Mom died. Not at the funeral. His eyes were red sometimes, but I never saw any tears. "I'm so sorry, Daze," he said. "I'm so sorry for what you went through. I should have been the one to find her. I'm sorry I was so late getting home that night. I'm sorry for not realizing . . . I thought she was doing better. I didn't know how bad it was. When she first went to the hospital it was because she'd slapped you, and she couldn't stand that she'd lost control like that because she loved you so much. . . ."

I flinched, burying my face in Mom's hair. "It was an accident," I murmured. "She didn't mean to." I wrapped my arms tighter around Mom. "She didn't mean to."

"None of us thought she would take her own life, Daze. Not me. Not the doctors. She hid it too well. "

✦ ✦ ✦

It's funny how dead objects are the ones that are forever, or a long time at least. Living things like people and animals and plants have a limited time. One of the defining qualities of being alive is that you won't always be. Being dead is the normal state of things. Life is the aberration.

The head, the thing I was holding on my lap, was a dead object. It wouldn't die, but it was never alive, either.

"I thought I was going crazy," I whispered. "When I kept hearing Mom's voice. Because there was something crazy in my head that made me hope she wasn't dead after all, that it was all a mistake somehow."

"I'm sorry . . ."

Something in me snapped. "You should be sorry! You built a robot Mom!"

Dad reached out, but I flinched away from him. "I didn't plan it like that," he said. "I just—I was working on an android. I wanted to make a real-looking android head. I already had her voice. Your mom's face . . . I knew it better than anyone's. It seemed a logical starting point. Then when she—it—had her voice, her smile . . . I couldn't take it back. I didn't know how to—how to end it."

"Then you met Sharon, and boom, Mom goes into the basement. The Graveyard!"

Dad's elbows were on his knees. His hands covered his face. "Was that why you took the head?"

"She was gone. You'd thrown her away!"

"I'd put her in temporary storage. I was going to take her apart and create a new face, a new voice simulator. Because attachment to an android head that looks and sounds like your mom was not good for me." He sat up straight. "And it's definitely not good for you, honey."

I held Mom closer. Her nose dug into my ribs. "You can't take her apart. It would be like her dying all over again."

Dad groaned. "Oh, honey. People only die once. And that's often enough."

"You brought Mom back to life. And now you want to kill her!"

Dad's voice was breaking up. "Daze . . ."

"Don't tell me, I need more therapy."

"I think we both do."

"Fine. You're not taking Mom away from me."

"This isn't your mother, Daze."

"It's the next best thing!"

Dad sighed deeply. He looked at my hands, white with the effort of holding Mom. "Daze, sweetie, you're holding a piece of technology. It's got circuits and wires and sophisticated programming. It's a prototype of a talking robot. It's got skin made of rubber and plastic, hair made of polypropylene."

"Stop it!" I wanted to cover my ears, but that would mean letting go of Mom, and the minute I did, Dad would grab her and she'd be gone forever.

"Without the program in my computer, this head is useless. It won't move, won't talk."

"Yes, she will. I have the program," I said. I snatched the memory key off the desk and put it around my neck again. "I have it on here, and backups all over the place. You'll never find them all. See? You can't take her away from me."

"She has only a limited set of responses, a heuristic net that is extremely limited. If you've talked to her—to *it*—you know that it's nothing like your mom. You've got to know that, Daze."

"We've talked," I said. "We've talked a lot."

"The program repeats what you say, rephrases it so it sounds natural. It has a lot of one-syllable responses that can also sound natural. It doesn't understand what you say, Daze. It grabs a word here and a word there, and it responds within the limits of its programming. It doesn't understand anything. It doesn't feel anything. And it's never going to be a mother to you. It's never going to tell you the things you want your mother to say."

I cursed my ears. They were badly designed. They should come with a closing mechanism, like our eyes. It wasn't fair that we could close our eyes if we didn't want to see something, but we couldn't close our ears if we didn't want to hear something. Even when I tried to recite multiplication tables in my head, Dad's words still penetrated and zoomed all through my brain.

And they hurt. Because they were true, and I knew it. Deep down I'd always known it.

"Daze." Dad's hand covered my hand on Mom's head, squeezed it. "I know how hard this has been on you. But we have to get past this. That thing is not your mother. It's a pile of electronics and motors and wires."

I looked down at Mom's hair. Something in me gave way. "I know," I whispered.

"You have to—You do?"

I nodded. "Yes, I do. She's dead. Just like Mom. Dead. I think we should bury her in Mom's grave."

"Bury her?" Dad sounded horrified. "We can't do that."

"What else do we do with her?"

"I thought I'd replace the face and voice—"

"Mom's not recyclable!"

"It's a prototype, Daze. I never should have built it to look like your mother in the first place, but I don't want to throw all that work away, either."

"Not throw away," I said tightly. "She should be buried. Mom should be in the grave with Mom."

"Do you know how absurd that sounded?" He looked at Dr. Alison. "Back me up here. Doesn't that sound absurd?"

Dr. Alison held up her hands. "The two of you are doing fine. Keep talking."

"I don't care if it's absurd!" I yelled. "It's where she belongs!"

"It's out of the question. It's not your mom, Daze. It's hardware. It's not getting a burial. It wouldn't be respectful to your mother's memory."

"You're not ripping her face off and putting another one on! I won't let you do that to her!"

Dad leaned back. He gestured at Dr. Alison. "Okay. We've reached an impasse. Help us out, will you?"

"Well. It's apparent that we need closure," Dr. Alison said.

I rolled my eyes. "*We?* You're not the one with your mom's android head on your lap!"

"I think you two need to compromise. Daze, don't you think your dad is right about your mother's grave being for your mother?"

I shrugged, and then I reluctantly nodded.

"And Steve, I think your daughter is right. Simply replacing the face and voice would not achieve closure for Daze. Don't you agree that she—this thing—needs to be gone for good?"

Dad and I fell silent. Then we looked at each other, now in alliance against Dr. Alison.

"What do you suggest?" Dad asked uneasily.

"I don't know." Dr. Alison rubbed her forehead. "How would you feel about the two of you disassembling her completely? Both of you?"

"But . . . ," Dad and I said simultaneously after a shocked silence. I was shocked enough that Dr. Alison managed to pull Mom out of my arms. She held Mom on her lap and traced a finger around Mom's eyes. I recoiled, didn't want to look. The skin around Mom's eyes was loose. It was necessary for flexibility, so her eyes could move and imitate all sorts of facial expressions.

"See? Look at this. It's a mask, a wig, hardware, and software."

"Um," I muttered, not looking.

"Look at her carefully, Daze. Try to see all the ways she's different from your mom."

Reluctantly I looked. Then I stared, really stared. And the longer I stared, the more things I noticed. Not only things I'd been refusing to see all this time, but also things I'd seen but told myself didn't matter. Not just the obvious ones, like the gaps between her eyes and the skin around them, or the teeth that were just paint, or the ears that looked nothing like human ears. I also noticed the colors, the shapes, the texture—it was all wrong.

The whole thing resembled my mom, like a bad painting maybe.

The individual bits looked like no one at all.

13

The cemetery smelled of autumn already. The leaves had just started to change colors. I hadn't been here for months. Not since I discovered the secret in Dad's workshop.

"We didn't get to say good-bye," Dad said when we'd sat in the grass next to the grave for a while. The angel had a gray tinge. I hadn't cleaned it in ages. "Doesn't seem fair, does it? It doesn't seem fair that she didn't even allow us to say good-bye."

I clenched my jaw. Tightened my grasp on the head through the leather of my backpack.

"I was angry for a long time, Daze. First I was sad and horrified, then I was angry, so incredibly angry. I didn't want to see her picture anywhere. I didn't want to talk about her. I didn't want to remember her at all, even the good times. And then, when the anger faded, I felt guilty. So guilty it hurt a million times more than before."

I tucked the backpack under my knees and bent over so I could cover my ears with my hands if I needed to.

"You're a good kid, Daze. The best. Your mom loved you. We can't ever understand why she did what she did, but it wasn't because we weren't good enough."

"You don't know that."

"I do know that, honey. It wasn't our fault."

I remembered when Mom went to the hospital for the first time. There was no explanation at first, just that Mom was away for the night. I guess Dad didn't know what to say. Then the next day he sat me down and explained that Mom was sick, that she would be at the hospital for a while, to get better. My eyes filled, and I remembered seeing Dad through a watery haze while something hard and cold and scary tightened in my chest.

"Is Mommy going to die?"

"No, honey." He'd smiled reassuringly, swept a thumb over my cheeks, flicking my tears away. "Don't worry. It's not that kind of an illness."

"You know, Dr. Alison thinks you never allowed yourself to be angry. Not at me, not at your mother."

I picked a leaf from the ground, felt it crumple when I closed my fist around it. "I'm not angry. I think she expected me to beat dolls with a hammer or something. If you ask me, therapists breed psychopaths."

"It's okay to be angry at your mom, Daze. It's natural. And for God's sake, it's okay to be angry at me. I can take it."

"I'm not angry at anyone!"

"Daze, your mom killed herself. And you found her. It feels like she chose to leave us. That she chose to abandon us. And that she didn't care what happened after she was gone. It's okay to be angry."

"I'm not angry!" I said through gritted teeth. "Quit the stupid angry talk!"

"I know it was scary when your mother was angry, but that was different. There were so many warning signs, but I didn't know—I didn't know how bad it was."

"She was a great mom. For a long time she was a great mom. But she hated it when Ryan cried," I said jerkily. "And then she started hating it when I—when I—"

Wanted a hug, I needed to say. But I couldn't. Because it

was childish and silly. Because I still didn't understand why Mom hadn't wanted to give me a hug when I needed one, and why she'd pushed me away when I thought she needed one, because I was little and stupid back then and I thought hugs fixed almost everything.

"Yes," Dad said. "She couldn't cope. And it made her angry and sad and hopeless. So she pushed us away. All of us. It wasn't our fault. It wasn't anything we did or didn't do."

"I think suicide should be illegal."

A small, sad smile flickered across Dad's face. "It was, once. In some places, those who attempted suicide got the death penalty."

"Well, that's not helpful!"

"No, it's not," Dad agreed.

"It's pretty stupid, actually."

I looked up. It was already winter on the mountaintops. Soon we'd have snow. The angel would have a soft white coat and a hat. Another Christmas without Mom.

I stretched my legs. The head felt hard and dead under my calves. It didn't belong here. I traced the carved rose on the headstone with two fingers, wiped some dirt off the angel's hair.

"I think Dr. Alison is right," I said. "I think we should

take her—it—apart. Completely apart. Together. It's the only way."

Dad nodded slowly. "I agree."

"Will you build a different one? Another android project?"

"I don't know. Maybe later. Much later, I think."

I leaned my head against Dad's shoulder. "Yes. I think that would be good. Much later."

"Maybe it's time to recycle your mother's things, too," Dad said. "We should go through her clothes and all that stuff in the basement. You and Ryan can keep whatever you want, but I think it's time to donate the rest to charity."

I nodded. I closed my eyes and saw Mom's face. A smile hovering over me when she tucked me into bed. A hand on my forehead, checking for fever. The frozen grin of the head was no longer polluting the memory, her eyes were warm and alive, her smile free of the motors, her laughter rich and happy, without the hollow speaker sound.

An image of water, water everywhere, filled my head. I opened my eyes to get rid of the pictures. I'd never forget that, either. I'd never understand, and maybe I'd never forgive.

I closed my eyes again and focused on replacing the bad images with the good ones. I thought about the coloring books and crayons I got every time I was sick, the way she always kissed my forehead when I left for school. I thought about counting stars before bedtime, of her tossing popcorn and catching it in her mouth, the burnt taste of cookies she made while distracted by her favorite TV shows, the way she'd hummed while she nursed Ryan.

My throat tightened, and behind my closed eyelids, tears welled up, more and more and more, until they burst out with the force of a tropical rainstorm. I heard grass crackle as Dad moved, felt his arms come around me, and I tangled my arms around his neck and buried my face in the soft material of his shirt.

Maybe I didn't need to understand and forgive. I just needed to remember.